Praise for Jill Ciment's

HEROIC MEASURES

"If ever there was a book I would nominate for bestseller-dom it's *Heroic Measures*. It's smart and funny and completely surprising. I've already bought a copy for everyone I know and I suggest you do the same. I loved every page."   —Ann Patchett

"It all sounds so ordinary—dogs get sick; people want to move—yet in Ms. Ciment's delicate hands, these characters become heroic in their small ways."
                —*The Wall Street Journal* (a summer reading pick)

"A wry, gentle gem of a novel. . . . [Ciment] paints the world of Alex and Ruth in gentle, exquisite detail. Yet never does their world seem too tiny to be of interest to us. Their efforts to retain some grace as they struggle for life's most basic desires—shelter and the safety of loved ones—are universal. . . . A lovely read."
                —*The Christian Science Monitor*

"It's funny what books stick in one's mind . . . with some lasting illumination the writer affords the reader. I doubt I'll walk through the East Village again without thinking of [*Heroic Measures*]."
                —Caitlin Macy, *The New York Times Book Review*

JILL CIMENT

HEROIC MEASURES

Jill Ciment was born in Montreal, Canada. She is the author of three novels, *The Tattoo Artist*, *Teeth of the Dog*, and *The Law of Falling Bodies*; a collection of stories, *Small Claims*; and a memoir, *Half a Life*. She has been awarded a National Endowment for the Arts Fellowship, a NEA Japan Fellowship Prize, two New York State Fellowships for the Arts, the Janet Heidinger Kafka Prize, and a Guggenheim Fellowship. Ciment is a professor at the University of Florida. She lives in Gainesville, Florida.

HEROIC
MEASURES

HEROIC MEASURES

A novel by

JILL CIMENT

Vintage Contemporaries
Vintage Books
A Division of Random House, Inc.
New York

FIRST VINTAGE CONTEMPORARIES EDITION, JUNE 2010

The Library of Congress has cataloged the Pantheon edition as follows:
Ciment, Jill.
Heroic measures / Jill Ciment.—1st ed.
p. cm.
1. Human-animal relationships—Fiction. 2. Missing persons—Fiction. 3. Television
feature stories—Fiction. 4. Manhattan (New York, N.Y.)—Fiction. I. Title.
PR9199.3.C299H27 2009
813'.54—dc22 2008034624

Vintage ISBN: 978-0-307-38678-6

www.vintagebooks.com

For Arnold

ACKNOWLEDGMENTS

The illuminated manuscript series attributed to my character, Alex, is based on *The FBI Files, a Collage Series* by Arnold Mesches.

The cartoon "Kvetch" on page 19 is by David Sipress.

The John Simon Guggenheim Memorial Foundation provided deeply appreciated financial support.

Friday Night

THE LADY WITH
THE PET DOG

IT IS THE HOUR WHEN THE LIGHT OVER THE sink, a fluorescent meant for washing dishes, suddenly usurps the fire of the dying sun and the kitchen window becomes a mirror, the moment every evening when Ruth realizes that her resolves are made of straw and Alex senses his age as a transitory chill.

Their *sun-flooded, eat-in kitchen* is prominently featured in the open house listing their realtor, Lily, is running in *The New York Times* tomorrow. When Lily first appraised their co-op, a five-flight walk-up in the East Village and suggested the asking price of nine hundred and ninety-nine thousand, Ruth felt the number bite her, like a needle, and enter her, like an intoxicating drug. As a child of the Depression, the word *millionaire* still held a magical spell, Fred Astaire dancing in top hat and tails. But the instant they signed Lily's contract, the headiness vanished. What were they doing selling their home of forty-five years? She didn't want to leave the city. They never cared about money before. Where would they go? She and Alex, never mind Dorothy, would be lost anywhere but New York.

Ruth looks across the kitchen table at Alex, seventy-eight years old, his white hair thick as a pelt, his white brows and beard stiff as wire, and envisions him mounting the five flights of stairs, the ample cavities of his eyes alive with determination, taking two steps at a time, his weekly test to prove to himself that he can still do it. But how long can he (or she for that matter) keep it up? With nine hundred and ninety-nine thousand, surely they can afford an elevator apartment somewhere in Manhattan.

When Alex first heard the asking price, he, too, felt weakened by the pull of the number's magnetism. His father, an immigrant shoe salesman, idolized millionaires as he had once revered rabbis in the old country, as men close to God. Ruth had initially called Lily just to see what their options were when the stairs became too much for them. But how could they turn down one million dollars? How could he? He had nothing to leave Ruth but his paintings, a legacy that often struck him as more of a burden than an asset. What will she do with all his artwork, fifty years of productivity, the fallout from his compulsion to keep painting no matter what? If she can't sell the paintings? If she can't sell the apartment when the time comes? She'll end up entombed in his work.

As preoccupied as they are with tomorrow's open house—Ruth has barely touched her chicken dinner, Alex has eaten most of his, but without pleasure or awareness—they still remember to set aside a few choice pieces for Dorothy.

From the doorway, Dorothy watches Ruth pick up Alex's plate, scrape his contribution into a bowl, add some morsels of her own, and then set the bowl on the tiled floor between their chairs. At twelve, eating is Dorothy's last great pleasure. Her dachshund face, mostly snout, is now completely white, whiter even than Alex's. She is missing two canines and three back molars. At her withers she stands eight inches tall, weighs ten pounds, two ounces. She tries to get up, but nothing happens. Her hind legs have turned to ice, burning ice. Without even knowing that she's doing it, she relieves herself on the tiles. She only knows that she has done so because of the odor; it smells sour and sick. She lets loose a shrill yelp.

Ruth looks in her direction, blinks for a moment or two, as if Dorothy had roused her from a trance. "Dorothy, have you wet yourself?" she asks, crossing the kitchen and bending over her.

Dorothy searches Ruth's eyes—mapped in wrinkles, putty-gray and magnified to omnipotence by thick glasses—for instructions. Should she stay put, or try to stand up again? What does Ruth think? If something truly bad had happened to her back half, wouldn't she see it in Ruth's stare, smell it on Ruth's skin? Ruth reeks of fear.

"It's okay, Dottie, we know you didn't mean to," Ruth murmurs. "Alex, something's terribly wrong with Dorothy."

Alex joins them on the floor, slips his hand under her belly, another under her chest. "I'm not going to hurt you," he says, gently lifting her out of her mess. When he sets her down on all fours, she sinks backward again, as if her ice legs had already melted in the fire. She shrieks.

"You're hurting her," Ruth says.

"I'm trying to find out what's wrong. She may have something stuck in her paw." Leaning closer, Alex examines her back feet. All she can feel, though, is smoldering numbness. "Walk away, Ruth. Pretend you're leaving. Open the door and call her."

"You think it's something in her paw? Dot can be such a little Sarah Bernhardt when she wants to be." Ruth unlocks the front door, holds up Dorothy's leash and collar, and waves them enthusiastically. "You want to go for a walk? Come on, Dottie, we'll go to the falafel stand."

Dorothy hears her tags rattling for her, but all she can manage is to scoot herself forward, an inch at a time.

"I'm calling the vet," Ruth says. Still holding the leash and collar, she hurries back into the kitchen. Dorothy fears she's coming back to yoke her to that lead, but Ruth steps over her and reaches for the phone.

"It's past six, no one will be there," Alex says. "Let's just go straight to the animal hospital."

Ruth puts down the phone.

"It may be nothing. Remember last year? Dot acted as if she was dying. Seven hundred dollars later we found out she had gas."

"Should we wait to see if she's better in the morning?" Ruth asks.

"I don't think we should wait."

"Is it safe to move her? Should I get her pillow?"

"It's too soft. She'll need more support."

"It's her back, isn't it?"

Alex looks around the kitchen and picks up the cutting board, while Ruth disappears into the bedroom and returns with Dorothy's tartan blanket and a couple of overcoats. Ruth swaddles Dorothy in the warm wool, while Alex helps her onto the board. Suddenly, whiffs of cheese, cow blood, chicken blood, bacon grease, parsley, peanut butter, and garlic permeate Dorothy's nostrils, but for once the smells bring her no pleasure.

Slipping their fingers under the board, Alex and Ruth lift her into the air and ferry her out the front door and down the hallway. At the precipice of the staircase, Dorothy begins to shake. Even under the best of circumstances, riding safely in Ruth's big purse or securely buttoned in Alex's overcoat, she fears the yawning, spiraling stairwell.

"How are we ever going to do this? I hate these stairs," Ruth says.

"You hold her, I'll hold the board under her," Alex says.

Ruth squeezes her with choking compassion, and the three of them start down the steps, Alex first, backward. Dorothy feels her blood swaying within her as Alex struggles to keep the board level. On the first landing, Ruth tightens her grip ever so slightly around Dorothy's middle, and the pain rages to life again. Dorothy first becomes aware of it as a color: orange. And a shape: sphere. Then the orange sphere explodes and the fire is no longer under her: Dorothy is inside the fire. She now resides in a conflagration so whole and absolute that it is a world unto itself. Nothing from her former existence matters. Her fear of stairs? Flashes away. Her insatiable appetite? Asphyxiates. Even her being caged in a burning body no longer concerns her. All that concerns Dorothy is the little sac of consciousness at the core of the blaze and what she keeps inside that sac: a carbon-hard nugget of trust that Alex and Ruth will know how to help her.

THE CO-OP'S LOBBY WON'T BE A SELLING point for Lily tomorrow. It's a narrow affair devoid of ornamentation, a passageway really, looking much as it did when the tenement was erected a hundred and six years ago to house fresh-off-the-boat immigrants, except for the new security system installed last year, a video camera mounted by the vestibule door. Ruth and Alex had voted against having a surveillance camera in their lobby, and not just because the monthly charges would rise. They didn't want their comings and goings spied on and recorded in the name of security ever again, even if, these days, they mostly ventured out to walk Dorothy. The original wrought-iron gate over the entry glass door, however, *is* something Lily will make sure every potential buyer notices: it harks back to a time when artisans, no matter how small the job, took pride in their craft.

Holding Dorothy between them, they push open the door. The street noise—sirens, horns, engines, bus brakes, whistles, shouts—is so penetrating, to Ruth at least, that it sounds as if all her tension has been given voice. For Alex, who doesn't yet realize he's forgotten his hearing aids in the rush to help Dorothy, the city's din, without the high and low notes, isn't so much piercing as keening. Traffic is frozen in both directions. A police helicopter hovers over the rooftops. A convoy of fire trucks, red lights whirring, is blocking the intersection at St. Mark's Place and Avenue A, but neither Ruth nor Alex see any fire or smell any smoke. Not even Dorothy smells smoke. Closing the door behind them, they assume it's another false alarm. Lately, if someone smells his neighbor burning toast, he panics and calls nine-one-one.

They carry Dorothy toward First Avenue hoping traffic will thaw out on the way and they'll catch a cab to the hospital, but when the signal up ahead changes, traffic only manages to jerk one car length forward despite the gunning rumblings and bullying horns. Standing in his restaurant doorway, facing the stalled procession of headlamps, Mr. Rahim, the falafel stand owner who always has a treat for Dorothy, holds up a hand-lettered cardboard sign:

Sahara Restaurant is Open for Business!!!!
Two Kebabs for the Price of One!!!
Complimentary Soda!!
United We Stand!

"What happened to Miss Dottie?" he asks, as soon as he sees it's Dorothy under the blanket.

"We think it's her back," Ruth says.

"Oh, poor thing."

"Is there a fire?" Alex asks.

Without taking his eyes off Dorothy, Mr. Rahim sighs and shrugs, a gesture of such private sorrow and public

skepticism it implies that even if the flames had been lick-
ing at his pant cuffs, he could no longer trust what is or
isn't real. "My wife calls to say there's a helicopter over our
roof, I should run home. But an off-duty policeman tells
me it's only a false alarm. Now my delivery boy hears on a
customer's TV that a gasoline truck is stuck in the Midtown Tunnel."

"He used the word *stuck*?" Alex asks.

"She just sat down and couldn't get up again," Ruth
says. "We're taking her to the hospital. She's freezing. We
have to go, Mr. Rahim."

They start across the icy pavement toward the first
available cab.

From his post on the sidewalk, Mr. Rahim watches
their slow progress as they thread between the snarled
bumpers, the old Jew in his black overcoat and red baseball cap, and his old owl-eyed wife in tears, and their sick
little dog. Mr. Rahim understands that they love the animal as if it were their own child, but there's something sad
and pathetic to him about such utter devotion to a beast,
though he's fond of the little dog himself. Mr. Rahim has
seven children. To love an animal as he loves his sons and
daughters strikes him as a form of blasphemy. The old husband and wife finally reach a taxi. Mr. Rahim can see by
the way they protect the poor creature as they climb inside
that the tenderness is genuine, even profound, and for a
moment, Mr. Rahim's strict hierarchical laws about which
animals are worthy of love and which are only worthy of
fondness are forgotten. "Good luck to you," he calls after
them.

In the taxi, Alex gives the driver, an Indian man with a

jackknife-size cross hanging from his rearview mirror, the hospital's address, fifty-four blocks north, while Ruth looks out her window at the solid lake of traffic. Between them on the backseat, supported by the cutting board and wrapped in the blanket, Dorothy moans. The sound is too faint for Alex to discern without his hearing aids, but Ruth hears it. Despite the trumpeting horns in front and in back of them, it's the only sound she hears. She and Alex have been responsible for this life since it was eight weeks old. Alex brought Dorothy home the day Ruth retired after three decades as a public school English teacher. Those first few nights tending to Dorothy's mystifying needs and constant demands had reminded Ruth of a Victorian novel in which the husband acquires an orphan for his graying childless wife to raise. Over the years, though, the dynamics of their threesome changed. For a time, Ruth and Alex were like two exasperated parents dealing with a rebellious toddler. Then, when puppyhood was behind them and Dorothy's neediness for Ruth turned to infatuation, she and Dorothy were like best girlfriends with a staid father chaperoning. Later, when Dorothy entered middle age and became gray and dignified, but inflexible and slightly hypochondriacal, Alex used to joke that he and Ruth were like illicit lovers with a maiden aunt sleeping in bed beside them. Of late, when Ruth woke in the night and saw the familiar forms sharing her bed—one white-bearded and supine, the other tiny, white-faced, and supine—their sleeping arrangements (Alex in the middle, she and Dorothy on either side) had begun to remind her of two old wives and a tired old polygamist. And now, stuck in traffic, it seems to Ruth that she and Alex are carrying the defenseless center of their marriage on a cutting board.

"How long has traffic been like this?" Alex asks the driver. "Do you know what's going on?"

"My last fare said there's a fire in the Midtown Tunnel, but my dispatcher says there's no fire."

"Did he say anything about a gasoline truck being stuck?"

"He says if I want my job I should keep driving."

Alex looks out his window. Cosmos Laundromat is open: the stout old proprietress is folding sheets. Lulu's Nails is open: the platinum blond Korean manicurist is smoking in the doorway. A first-story apartment window rises and a young woman's slender arm reaches through the bars to empty a DustBuster. Alex watches as the leavings fall at the same speed as snow. If something were really wrong, wouldn't people be panicking?

When Ruth looks out her window, the glass might as well be opaque. She's thinking about this morning when she and Dorothy had first stepped outside. Overnight, fresh ice had encrusted the stoop, the fire escape, the bricks and the ancient mortar between the bricks, the garbage cans shackled together in chains, the grills of air conditioners, and every branch of every tree growing out of a glistening wrought-iron corral. In the early light, the street looked tooled in silver, and she felt such tenderness for their neighborhood that she had to collect herself or she might start to cry: they were being wrenched away from everything they loved and knew just when their age demanded stability. She gently closed the ancient entry door behind her (lest the old glass break before the open house tomorrow) and took hold of the railing (lest she slip on the icy steps). You're acting like a frightened old woman. Why is old age synonymous with stability? Old age is anything but stable. And for the first time since they'd signed Lily's contract three days ago, the heady intoxication returned. Even if they couldn't afford Manhattan, with a million dollars, they could afford just about anywhere else—the Jersey shore, or that car-less island in North Carolina she saw advertised in the *New Yorker,* or Fort Myers, close to her sister. But she didn't want to be banished to South Florida where it was too hot to walk — neither of them had ever learned to drive—or to the Jersey Shore where they knew no one, or to that car-less island in middle of the ocean. How long can you stare at an ocean? And then, the idea that she and Alex, lifelong New Yorkers, were being squeezed out of their city because, even if someone wrote them a check for a million, they still might not be able to afford an elevator apartment large enough for Alex to paint in, had propelled her, like an angry push, down the stoop steps. Tethered to her by the leash, Dorothy had no choice but to clamber down the stairs behind her. Is that how Dorothy hurt her back? Why hadn't she thought to pick her up?

Alex taps his foot, jiggles his knee, as if anxiousness itself might impel the cab to go faster. For the past ten minutes, they've been stuck behind a crosstown bus at the intersection of Thirty-fourth Street and First Avenue. Though

Alex may not be able to hear Dorothy's moans, he's aware of them: Dorothy has shifted her weight and is panting heavily against him.

"Do you think Third might be faster?" he asks the driver.

"My dispatcher says I'm not paid to think."

Alex looks in the direction of Third Avenue. Thirty-fourth Street appears to be welded solid with cars and buses. He looks in the direction of the river. More fire trucks and squad cars are blocking the lanes. Television crews now choke the sidewalks. "Could you turn on the news?" he asks the driver.

The cabbie switches on the radio, but the station he tunes in sounds, to Alex's ears, as if it's being broadcast from under the East River. "Could you make it louder?" he asks.

Ruth stares at him. "Did you forget your hearing aids? Not tonight of all nights."

Alex now realizes that the low sorrowful keening he's been hearing ever since he stepped outside this evening is just a muted version of the real thing. He is unarmored. He won't be able tell which direction the sirens are coming from or heading to; he won't be alert to any alarming increases in the city's volume, but that's not all that worries him. He can negotiate New York deaf if he has to. It's the hospital. What if the nurses speak too softly or too fast? What if the doctor mumbles or has an accent? He'll have to ask Ruth to repeat what's wrong with Dorothy over and over again.

"There *is* a gasoline truck stuck in the Midtown," Ruth announces.

"At least there's no fire," the cabbie says.

"Police are evacuating the tunnel in both directions, people are abandoning their cars and running," she interprets the radio's faint mumbles for Alex. "Aren't we on top of the tunnel now?"

Alex, Ruth, and the driver all look down just as a crosstown bus grinds into motion and a passageway unlocks in the bulwark of cars. The taxi rushes through and once again, albeit slowly, they are rolling up First Avenue.

"The tanker jackknifed; it's blocking all in-bound lanes," Ruth continues. "Police don't know if it was an accident or if the driver swerved on purpose. The mayor is asking everyone to remain calm and to not drive into Manhattan tonight. Who would come into the city tonight?"

Five blocks short of the hospital, they jerk to a standstill again. Tunnel traffic is being detoured onto the Fifty-ninth Street Bridge. The old four-lane structure can't accommodate the overspill. Up ahead, signals change and change again, and nothing gives. Eventually even horns stop honking. Left and right, fares begin deserting their cabs to continue north on foot. They carry their belongings in their arms: cleaning, groceries, children, strollers, a full-length mirror with the price tag still on it.

"It's too cold for her," Ruth says.

"We have no choice."

Ruth doubles the blanket over Dorothy while Alex pays. Despite the urgency he feels to get Dorothy to the hospital, and the electric panic in the air, and the rumbling of fear under his feet (the low vibrations from thousands of trapped engines gunning in place), and the adrenaline pumping through his frame, preparing him for flight, Alex can't help himself, he asks the driver for a receipt.

"Driver's licenses? Picture IDs," says the guard, a moon-faced young man posted inside the overheated animal hospital's lobby, beside a metal detector.

Ruth and Alex are panting from the hurried, five-block journey, tear-blind from the cold. In the first blast of steam heat, Ruth feels Dorothy's shivering subside and her peculiar rigidity grow loose again. She releases her grip on the blanket, even though she's worried her grip is all that's holding Dorothy together, while Alex gently sets the cutting board on a card table near the guard. They produce their picture IDs—a gym membership card for Alex and a twenty-five-year-old teachers' union card for Ruth (at fifty-two, she had looked like Imogene Coco in thick glasses).

They pick up the board and ferry Dorothy through the metal detector, Alex first, backward. The buzzer sounds. They step back, lower Dorothy onto the card table again, and empty their pockets of keys and coins. They start through the electrified field once more, but the buzzer goes off again. Alex removes his wristwatch, Ruth hands the guard her purse so he can inspect its contents—pencils, a cell phone with two years' worth of flashing messages (neither Ruth or Alex know how to retrieve the messages), a cellophane bar code that has peeled off the back of her library card, a sandwich bag of dog treats. They pick up Dorothy one more time and try to cross the threshold, but the buzzer rings and rings.

"Can't you see she's in pain? Is this necessary?" Ruth asks.

"It's for security, ma'am."

"Who would blow up a hospital full of sick cats and dogs?"

Alex touches her sleeve: he's found the source of the alarm, the metal buckle on Dorothy's faux leopard collar. Ruth had bought the collar because she though it gave Dorothy a risqué, haughty look, an old dominatrix, say, whose specialty was biting. Ruth watches as Alex unclasps the buckle at the nape of Dorothy's neck with intimacy and caution, a husband removing his ill wife's necklace.

The emergency room's front desk is glassed-in, like an aquarium. The receptionist, a large powdery woman in a pink cardigan mottled with cat hairs, looks up over her half-glasses. "Name? Address? Phone number? Pet's name?"

"Dorothy," Alex answers.

At the mention of her name, Alex notices the blanket stir on the board. Under its hem, in a tent of ratty wool, Dorothy's one visible eye looks up at him.

"What's wrong with Dorothy this evening?"

The eye casts about to see who else knows her name, and for a moment, it seems to Alex that if he lifts the blanket, there will only be an enormous trusting eye beneath it. "She doesn't seem to be able to move her back legs," he says. With disbelief, he watches as the receptionist writes down *paraplegic*.

"Any other symptoms?"

"Isn't that enough?" Ruth says.

"How long has she been down?"

"It happened during dinner," Alex says.

"Take a seat. Someone will call you shortly."

"Please. It took us almost two hours to get here. It's an emergency," he says.

The receptionist makes a small lateral motion with her head and stares past him and Ruth and Dorothy with such deliberate, barefaced pity that he can't help but follow her gaze. In a row of plastic chairs facing the desk, sits a businessman and a Pomeranian, an old woman and a Chihuahua, and a Spanish lady and a Saint Bernard. The Pomeranian's left eye has somehow come loose; it dangles, as round and red as a maraschino cherry, from a tearing socket. The Chihuahua moans in a yellow towel. The Saint Bernard is swaying dramatically from side to side, as if the floor were pitching.

Alex and Ruth take the three empty chairs next to the Chihuahua's owner and place Dorothy on the seat between them.

"What's your baby in for?" the Chihuahua's owner asks.

"We think it's her back," Ruth says.

"I found her walking in circles this morning," the Chihuahua's owner whispers as if the two dogs might overhear her.

"Our vet says it's a fat deposit," the Saint Bernard's owner says, lifting the rocking behemoth's ear to reveal a mass the size of the Chihuahua. "Does this look like a fat deposit to you?" she asks. "Because I know my fat deposits. Trust me, *that's* not fat."

"She's blind now, but you'd never know it," the Chihuahua's owner continues. "We're both diabetic. We use the same brand of insulin; it makes life easier that way."

"Will Dorothy's owners please go to exam room one," the receptionist's voice floats out of a speaker in her glass enclosure.

At the announcement of her name, Dorothy rouses once again. This time Alex takes off the blanket. Neck rigid, back as bowed as an archway, tail crushed beneath her, hind legs folded at odd, disturbing angles, Dorothy still manages to look up at him with unsullied trust. He picks her up off the cutting board, and he and Ruth take her to exam room one. In his arms, she weighs no more than a game hen.

"They're our angels," the Chihuahua's owner calls after them.

The examining room contains only a metal table, two chairs, a clear plastic rack filled with drug brochures, a cartoon of a little dog, a stick, and an elderly couple scotch-taped to the back of the door (Man: *Fetch*. Little Dog: *Oy, I got a pain in my tail from wagging so much, my stomach hurts from that lousy dog food, when are we going for a walk already?* Woman: *He thinks you said "kvetch"*) and a forgotten X-ray clipped to a light box on the white wall. It doesn't take a doctor to read the film; a white mass fills most of the animal's lungs, though Alex can't tell what kind of animal it is: the lungs look human to him.

A medical student, a boy of about twenty-five holding a clipboard, comes in and closes the door behind him. "I'm going to take Dorothy's history, and then Dr. Rush is going to examine her."

"Should I put her on the table?" Alex asks.

"You can hold her for now," the student says. "Tell me what happened?"

"She may have hurt her back this morning running down the stoop," Ruth says.

Alex looks at her; her eyes are bright with tears. "Why didn't you tell me?" he asks.

"I didn't know anything was wrong until dinner. You don't think I would have told you?" Ruth turns to the medical student, "Normally, she gets to the table before us."

"We found her on the kitchen floor, sitting in her own urine," Alex says. "When I picked her up, she screamed. She doesn't seem to be able to move her back legs."

"We even pretended we were going to take her to the falafel stand," Ruth adds, "but she wouldn't come."

"How has her appetite been lately?"

"She didn't touch her breakfast today," Alex says.

"Any vomiting or diarrhea?"

"Last week."

"But it passed," Ruth adds. "We think it was the pâté."

"Any changes in behavior? Sleeping more? Not wanting to play?"

"She's been extremely nervous lately," Alex says.

"Everything scares her," Ruth adds. "Loud noises, sirens, strangers, even being left alone in the apartment for an hour or two. It's not like her; she's always been such a brave dog."

"The vet put her on Clomicalm," Alex explains.

"Any other medications?"

"Zubrin twenty-five milligrams, Soloxine for her arthritis, and Atopica for her rashes."

"Allergies?"

"Strawberries and coconut."

The doctor comes in. He's wearing a necktie patterned with cows, a whole herd. His face and neck are pitted with acne scars, making his blue eyes seem especially kind.

"You can put Dorothy on the table now," the medical student tells Alex.

"What did you do to yourself, little hot dog?" the doctor asks, introducing himself to Dorothy by offering her the back of his hand to sniff. Alex takes note of how gentle a hand it is, but Dorothy ignores it; she doesn't even seem aware that the doctor is there.

Without seeming to cause Dorothy any needless pain, the doctor palpates, prods, pokes, and listens. He uses his pencil's eraser to check her reflexes: her nerves are that small. He taps her withers; the front legs jump. He taps her hips: the back legs hang. Supporting her under her belly, he stands her up on all fours, and lets go. He watches as her hind end slowly sinks down, as if Dorothy were deflating. Next he puts her on the floor. "Call her," he says to them.

Alex walks to the far corner and faces Dorothy. He can sense that she, too, suspects the hopelessness of the test, but he can also see, by the alertness of her ears, that she will try her utmost to reach him. He beckons to her.

Dorothy scratches at the linoleum with her blunt nails, belly crawling to Alex, her back legs dragging behind, like knotted rags.

"I can't watch," Ruth says and escapes into the hall, leaving Alex to suffer Dorothy's ordeal alone.

The doctor stops the test and calls Ruth back inside. "It's most likely a ruptured disc," he tells them. "But it could also be neurological. It might even be a tumor. We won't know until we x-ray her."

"But you think it's only a slipped disc?" Ruth asks, hopeful.

"Ruptured. That would be my guess. It's fairly common in chondrodystrophoids, short-legged, long-bodied dogs. Dwarfs, really. Imagine a suspension bridge without the cables. It's only a guess, though, until I see X-rays." He pats Dorothy's head and whispers, "Don't worry, we have a special wiener x-ray machine." He disappears with her down the hallway.

"You can wait here," the medical student tells them.

Alex and Ruth sit down on the two chairs.

"Do you think a ruptured disc is fixable?" Ruth asks.

"I hope so."

"Why didn't you tell me she hadn't eaten her breakfast?"

"I didn't think it was important," Alex says, but even as he says it, he realizes it's not true. He, too, should have known that something was wrong with Dorothy this morning. He found her trembling on his studio floor soon after Ruth and she had returned from her walk. Assuming she was cold, he picked her up, tucked her into his bathrobe, and stroked her fur until her shivering ceased. In his arms, next to his skin, Dorothy soon began sighing, long, deep exhalations of such contentment he ached to join in, to give voice to his own exhaustion and yearnings, to just breath in and out and not have to think about him and Ruth starting over. Now he realizes that the moans issuing from Dorothy weren't sighs of contentment; they were whimpers of pain. He'd been wearing his hearing aids this morning: he should have discerned the difference.

"How long does an X-ray take?" Ruth asks, hoarse. To distract her and himself, he reaches for a handful of drug brochures, and shows her the picture on the top one, a picket line of cartoon cats holding up protest signs. He reads the caption aloud, *"Join the Revolution. In the campaign against parasites, we know our only solution is Revolution."*

"Do you think the truck crashed on purpose? Is it rigged to explode?" Ruth asks.

"I hope not," he says, and turns to the next brochure, a bulldog grinning in a dentist's chair: *Clavamox keeps more than your pet's teeth from decaying.* The dog's teeth are whiter than his.

"Should we have sold last year, Alex? Did we wait too long?"

The doctor returns: he isn't carrying Dorothy. No one has to tell Alex this isn't a good sign.

"It's as we suspected," the doctor tells them, "Dorothy has suffered a ruptured disc. We'd like to start her on prednisone and see how she does during the next twelve to twenty-four hours. Some dogs respond extremely well to the steroid therapy."

"The ones that don't?" Alex asks.

"The spinal cord is very fragile. Once it's damaged, it can't be repaired. Dogs are remarkably adaptable, though. With the help of wheels, I've seen dogs with full paralysis chase balls. They accept their fate with a lot more peace than we do. The paralysis sometimes seems harder on the owners than their pets."

Does he really believe that? Alex thinks.

"The rupture occurred between T-13 and L-1, about two-thirds down her spine. At the moment, she's lost mobility in her hind legs, but she's still experiencing deep pain."

"Can't you do something for the pain?" Ruth asks.

"We *want* her to experience deep pain. It means her spinal cord has at least one live wire running through it. As long as she feels pain, we have hope."

Pain equals hope? Ruth thinks.

"If she doesn't get worse during the night, we'll continue the course of steroids and see how she does."

"If she gets worse?" Alex asks.

"Surgery. We perform a hemilaminectomy as soon as we can schedule one, remove any bone and disc material pressing against the cord. But even with surgery, the prognosis still depends on how acute the rupture is. You should also know that the surgery carries risks, especially at Dorothy's age. Surgery is an option you might have to consider, though. Meanwhile, let's hope the steroids work. A nurse will phone you if there are any changes."

In the waiting room, the cutting board and blanket are just where they left them.

They lay out all their credit cards on the cashier's desk. A card trick, Ruth thinks, shuffling through them in search of a magical one that still has enough balance left to conjure up payment for Dorothy's procedures—steroid treatments, and if those don't work, a hyperosmolar agent, and if that doesn't work, a myelogram and hemilaminectomy. The costs are listed on a permission form she and Alex have been asked to sign. Dorothy's back could run to the thousands. Ruth signs for everything and anything, and then hands the form to Alex. She watches him as he initials, from all Dorothy's options, the one that harbingers the worst possible scenario: *Do Not Resuscitate.*

"What are you doing?" she demands.

"At her age, I don't think we should let them take heroic measures."

"That's not your decision to make alone. When were you planning on telling me? After they pull the plug?"

"Let them try the steroids, even surgery if it comes to that. But when they open her, if it looks like she'll never walk again, maybe we should ask the doctor not to wake her. Our Dot's had a good life. If she can't walk, she'll need to be helped to the bathroom. Every time. She might even be incontinent. I don't know if we should put her through this, if she would want us to."

"I don't mind helping her."

"She might mind."

IT'S NOT AS IF DOROTHY DOESN'T KNOW where she is, she's seen her share of doctors: when she swallowed a pound of Brie at Alex's gallery opening, tore off her nail on a hook rug, had a seizure at the falafel stand, sampled rat poison at the park, was attacked by a pack of Chihuahuas; the time a stranger with a kind face beckoned her to him with the promise of salami, then kicked her in the ribs for no reason; and just last month, when the anxiety of being left alone in the apartment became too much for her again, particularly as dusk fell and nocturnal shadows grew menacing, and her sense of loneliness and old age became inseparable. She barked until she heard Ruth and Alex inside the building, howled for them to hurry up the staircase, and when they finally appeared, couldn't stop whimpering. They brought her to the doctor's the next day.

But Alex and Ruth have never before rushed her to a place like this. This is a skyscraper-size warren of illness and emergencies. Every passageway the nurse carries her through smells of blood and urine, and she's so tired from the pain, so ready to let go of it and nestle inside woolly sleep. But she stays vigilant, keeping track of every odor, and the saturation of the odor's age, and the direction of its musk, so that she can find her way back to Alex and Ruth.

In a small room lined with cages, the nurse sets her atop a steel gurney and wheels her under a bright lamp. The nape of her neck is shaved. Clumps of her fur land all around her. Something sharp and cold jabs her between the shoulder blades and she screams more in fear than in pain: after the orange explosion, she has a whole other appreciation of pain. When she's able to turn her head, she sees she's been tethered to a bag of liquid. The bag is almost as big as she is. Now, even if she manages to escape the nurse and get down from the table, how will she find the strength to drag both her hind legs *and* the bag of liquid in search of home?

She and the bag are put in a cage. To her right, in a separate cell, something moans under a yellow towel, and to her left, something whimpers through the bars. Dorothy has no patience for the suffering of other dogs. She closes her eyes. Whenever she hears human voices, though, she rouses herself. Maybe Alex and Ruth have come for her?

THE HOSPITAL'S AUTOMATED GLASS DOORS spring open. The night air is now so arctic and still, Ruth half expects the city to sound muted; the noise assaults her like fists. When Alex hears the dull din again, he's almost relieved: any noise but the muffled despair of the hospital.

Alex carries the board, Ruth the blanket. There's no point in looking for a taxi; the whole East Side is still log-jammed. They could walk home faster, if it wasn't so cold and far, and they weren't so exhausted and sad.

"Should we try the subway?" Alex asks.

"I'm not riding in any tunnels tonight," Ruth says.

Near the bus stop, a woman dressed in a fur coat and house slippers comes out her lobby door and peers down Second Avenue. Brake lights recede to infinity. A news helicopter circles overhead. Police part traffic to let a caravan of armored FBI trucks through. "Do you know what's going on?" she asks Alex and Ruth. "My cable's out."

"We've been at the animal hospital for the past couple of hours," Alex says.

"Our dog might be paralyzed," Ruth blurts out, lest Dorothy's tragedy already be forgotten in the city's crisis.

"All we know is the Midtown Tunnel has been closed," Alex tells her.

"A tanker truck crashed inside," Ruth adds. "We don't know if it was an accident or if the driver swerved on purpose."

"Do you think that's why my cable's out?"

Next to the bus stop is a newspaper kiosk, the headlines already old news. Behind a curtain of tabloids hanging from clothespins, the vendor stares at a television no bigger than a toaster. The screen is entirely phosphorescent green, except for a local news channel's logo, and what Alex and Ruth assume are the tanker's headlamps glowing in the belly of the tunnel. They watch as the yellow orbs grow bigger, brighter, sharper, and closer.

"Who's operating the camera?" Alex asks the vender.

"The FBI. It's an unmanned bomb robot with a night-vision camera mounted on top," he answers, without taking his eyes off the set.

Ruth and Alex can now see a faint shape behind the headlights, something more suggested than real—a ghostly relic, sunken tonnage, a danger that's been down in that tunnel for decades rather than hours.

"They think there's a bomb?" Alex asks.

The vendor shrugs. "They're still looking for the driver."

"Is he in the truck?"

"The tank holds ten thousand gallons of gasoline. Would you stay inside that truck?"

Stuffy, humid, alive with perfumes and must, the downtown bus is standing-room-only. The crowd separates them, Ruth to the rear, Alex up front near the trio of seats set aside for the handicapped and the elderly. He grabs a strap as the bus releases its airbrakes. A middle-aged woman offers him her seat, a gesture he normally finds demeaning, but tonight seems kind beyond words. He rests the cutting board across his lap and closes his eyes, just for a second or two. Once he shuts them, though, he realizes he hasn't the will to open them. Heat pours up through the floor vents. The bus sways. The weight of the cutting board is like a blanket. All this should put him to sleep, but it's not exhaustion he feels, it's relief, primal burning relief, as when you open a blister.

He's as terrified as the next man about what might be down in that tunnel, but he can't deny the exquisite rush of release he feels. He's been granted a temporary reprieve. He won't have to suffer house hunters in his studio tomorrow—stepping around piles of drawings, setting their wet gloves on his work bench, a surface he keeps as clean and neat as an operating table; strangers measuring walls thick with sketches—disturbing the fragile alchemy of chaos and sterility he needs for his work. He's been covering these walls with his imagery for almost half a century, as methodically as a clam secretes its essence to make its shell. When Lily had first peered into his studio during the appraisal, she proclaimed it would make a perfect nursery.

Ruth suggested he take Polaroids of his studio so that when they move, they'll be able to set up his new studio—wherever that may be—exactly like the old one.

How can he explain to her that it isn't just the room, it's also the routine, the uniformity of the airshaft light, the predictability of the clanging radiator. The wretched monotony is needed for wild exuberance, the safety of going crazy in a padded cell. His latest creations are illuminated manuscripts he's been working on for the past year. As monks once illustrated the Bible with gold leaf and devotion, he is illuminating the seven-hundred-and-fifty-page file that the FBI had kept on Ruth and him during the heyday of the cold war. Initial showings of the manuscript pages have garnered him just enough attention from the art world to offer promise, though at his age, he isn't exactly sure what promise means anymore.

He'd prefer putting off their move—a disruption, in all likelihood, that might cost him months—until he is at least halfway finished with his tome, the point of no return, but how can he ask Ruth to wait? He is only on page fifty-one of seven hundred and fifty. And now, as long as the danger remains in the tunnel, the question is moot. Who shops for a nursery during a red alert?

They disembark at St. Mark's Place. Mr. Rahim is rolling down his metal shutter for the night. He sees them before they see him, the old husband gripping the empty cutting board and his old wife clutching the shabby blanket. They look, to Mr. Rahim, like refugees. "How's Miss Dottie?" he asks.

"She might need surgery," Ruth says.

"Any news about the truck?" Alex asks.

"The robot's found nothing so far, but the FBI is saying the bomb may be *inside* the tank. It's an Exxon truck. No one knows where the driver is. Police aren't even sure the driver was behind the wheel when it crashed. He may have been hijacked. A police sketch of a man witnesses saw fleeing the truck is all over the TV. My wife phones to say she thinks it's our super. When did our super, who can't fix the boiler, learn to drive a tanker truck?"

Mr. Rahim glances over at the wife. Her bottle-thick glasses are dusted with hoarfrost. Even so, he can see her eyes are red-rimmed. "Is the surgery dangerous?" he asks her.

"At Dorothy's age, everything is risky."

The five flights of stairs are a drawback, but not a deal breaker, according to Lily. "The East Village is a young person's neighborhood these days, edgy and energetic. The stairs can even be an asset; they keep the monthly charges low."

Ruth looks up at the ascending steps. It's like climbing to the top of a bell tower. She could barely summon the strength to walk home from the bus stop, but he's already started up, taking two treads at a time. The walls echo and amplify; she hears him breathing hard, sighing, his footfalls increasingly leaden. But he doesn't slow down. What does his stupid test prove? Does he think he can outrun death? Does he think if he doesn't waste time, time won't waste him?

Alex is already in the apartment when she finally catches up. She reaches for the light switch. Dorothy's rubber mailman, her squeaky hot dog, her tennis ball lay scattered on the floor, her leash and winter sweater hang on a hook. In the kitchen, her untouched bowl waits between their chairs, her mess lays pooled on the tiles.

Ruth sheds her coat, picks up a roll of paper towels and cleanser, gets on her knees, and wipes up the mess with an intensity and vigor that rivals Alex's sprint up the steps. She clears the table, throws the leftover chicken into the garbage, rinses the plates, and stacks them in the dishwasher.

"Ruth," Alex says, "we can clean up tomorrow."

"When? The open house starts at nine."

"I don't think anyone's going house hunting tomorrow."

"You don't know that."

"Would you buy an apartment this weekend?"

She wipes the table and counters, gets out the broom and sweeps. She can't stop herself anymore than he could. Does she think if her floor is swept, the young and the energetic won't notice the new water stain on the ceiling, the missing knob on the twenty-year-old stove? Does she think she can fool death with cleanser and paper towels? Out of the corner of her eye she sees Alex is trying to help. He retrieves the cutting board from the hall, runs hot water over it, soaps, rinses, wipes, and then sets it atop the counter. Casting him a look of disbelief, she removes the cutting board and leans it against the garbage pail to be thrown out with the chicken.

The phone rings. Something's happened to Dorothy! Ruth grabs the receiver and crushes it to her ear.

"Sorry to call so late, but I wanted to alert you that I'm bringing a couple by at eight-thirty."

From the other side of the kitchen, Alex mouths, Is it the hospital? She shakes her head no. "What about the tunnel?" she asks Lily.

"I closed on a Tribeca loft the day after Nine Eleven.

We might not get the hordes we want, but we'll get the serious ones, and that will work in our favor."

Ruth hangs up. "Lily's bringing a couple by at eight-thirty. The open house *is* on."

Alex hunts for the remote to turn on the news, while Ruth searches for her glasses. She must have taken them off to wash the dishes, but they're not next to the sink. Without her glasses, Ruth feels naked, more than just undressed, soulless. She's been wearing glasses since she was nine years old. Before glasses her childhood, a ten-block area around King's Highway in Brooklyn, had been but light and shadow. When she slipped on her first pair, thick as table-glass, and looked out the optician's window, she saw that the foaming horse harnessed to a rag wagon, the beggar picking up cigarette butts, the beat cop, the newspaper boy fanning himself with headlines, the men waiting in line for soup, the blur of humanity at the nadir of the Depression, was actually made up of individual faces, each face, including the horse's, expressing such blatant defeat or rage or worry or hunger or bewilderment that Ruth felt as if she had caught them at their most private moments. Ruth believes that initial shock of clarity awoke in her the first stirring of compassion, that, in many ways, her glasses tell her story.

Her first frames were thick-rimmed and brown, the least expensive in the shop, chosen by her mother. Even seeing clearly in those years struck her mother, a Russian immigrant with four other children to feed, as an extravagance.

Her next pair, tiny round wire rims, Ruth chose herself. At sixteen, short, with her mother's ample breasts and her father's wild hair, she hoped the frames' austerity lent her the seriousness with which she yearned to be taken. All the nearsighted Jewish girls in the young socialist club wore round wire frames.

She was wearing black horn-rims when she first met Alex. He was one of the square-shouldered, chain-smoking, intense, wry veterans crowding City College after the war. He wore paint-splattered army pants and smoked French cigarettes in class. He wasn't afraid to show disdain when he didn't agree with professors or reverence when he did. Taking a chair beside him one afternoon as the lights dimmed for an art history slide lecture, Ruth spent the hour studying him; his eyes, caverns of intensity under stiff black brows. He looked as if he was staring into a sun rather than at an example of somber Dutch realism. She invited him to a Henry Wallace for President rally that evening—she was recording secretary of the Progressive Party campus chapter. He was standing by the classroom door, the last to leave. When Ruth was nervous, she imploded behind her glasses. He gently slid them off, studied her naked eyes with the same intensity she'd witnessed all afternoon, and then slid them back on again. It was the sexiest thing that had ever happened to her. A week later, almost to the day, she was lying nude in his bed, her glasses on the floor.

She and Alex chose her next frames—red, cat-eye, urban, the height of beatnik fashion. She was wearing them her first day of teaching, the week they purchased the apartment for five grand (sixty dollars and seventy-eight cents a month on the GI Bill). Most of their friends—painters, fellow travelers, the sculptress and her war-damaged husband, the musician couple who chain-smoked reefer—were moving to the suburbs and having children, diaper pins clamped between lips where jays once slanted. Sitting with them in their spanking-new treeless box houses, in toy-strewn living rooms that smelled of sour milk and talc, holding squirming infants in her arms, Ruth acted disappointed that she hadn't yet gotten pregnant, but truthfully, all she felt was relief.

Now, near blind as she hunts for her glasses (thick, round, brown, a piece of translucent tape reinforcing the left temple), the repercussion of their decision (if that's what it was) to remain childless and free is inescapable. She and Alex have no one but each other—two specks of dust soon to be scattered to the universe. She gropes behind the microwave and finally feels her thick-rimmed frames. How did her glasses get there?

Alex presses the red button in the upper-left-hand corner of the remote control, careful not to graze any other button lest he accidentally deprogram the cable box as he did last month. It took him and Ruth the better part of a weekend to reprogram it.

He inserts his hearing aids and sits on the sofa across from the TV. Ruth slips on her glasses and sits beside him.

A gyrating cube with the network's logo spins toward them. A ticker tape of stock quotes, sport's scores, and headlines scroll across the bottom of the screen. The news-caster's face fills the rest. His eyes resemble a basset hound's. "Here's how our viewer's responded to tonight's polling question. If you were in New York City, would you stop using the tunnels and bridges for the next few days? Forty-eight percent of you say yes, forty-two percent say no, and ten percent are undecided."

"There's nothing new," Ruth says. "They don't know anything. They're filling time."

"How do you know? It says LIVE. You're the one who told me if it says LIVE, something's going on."

"They're onto LIVE. They know all about LIVE. Nowadays, all LIVE means is that the newscaster isn't dead."

The phone rings again. They both look down at the extension on the coffee table. Alex picks it up. All he hears, though, is a dial tone, yet it won't stop ringing. "It's dead."

"It's the cell phone!" Ruth says, foraging through her purse. She presses the ringing instrument to her ear. By her expression—eyes closed, mouth a wide slot of darkness, forehead painfully taut, as if someone is pulling her hair— Alex doesn't need to ask who it is.

She covers the mouthpiece. "Dorothy can't feel pain any longer. They don't think the steroids are going to work. She needs the surgery. They have to perform a test first to see where to operate. The dye can cause seizures. The test could kill her. She'll have it around seven; if she's operable she'll go right to surgery. They need to speak to you. We put it on your credit card." She hands him the cell phone.

Even under the best of circumstances—the satellite is overhead, the TV is mute—he can barely make out what anyone says to him on the cell phone. A woman's voice crackles *three hundred* or *three thousand,* he can't tell. He turns to Ruth, but she's risen off the sofa, her back to him. Her glasses remain on the armrest, the lenses catching the kitchen's fluorescent glow, concentrating it into two tiny suns.

"We'll authorize the test," Alex tells the woman, "but please have Dr. Rush call us on our land line with the test results. We want to talk to him *before* the surgery." He closes the phone, puts it back in her purse.

"He talked about a wheelchair of some sort," Ruth says. "He said the dogs adjust better than their owners."

"Did you believe him?"

"No."

She sits down again, pulls a tissue from her purse, wipes her eyes, and then crushes the sodden wad in her fist, as if she were trying to compress it into a diamond. In a voice as calm as he can manage, he says, "She's one tough old dame, Ruth. She might surprise us."

He takes her hand, and they sit side by side in the television's volatile, liquid light. The newscaster is now interviewing a robotics expert who explains, in a droning monotone, how an aqua-bomb robot can enter a ten-thousand-gallon gasoline tank and maneuver through highly flammable liquid without destabilizing the environment. "She's called a Robo-eel. She uses the undulating motions of an eel to keep friction to a minimum."

Ruth is right, there's nothing new.

Without even knowing that he's doing it, Alex nods off, catches himself, and sits upright. He doesn't want to leave Ruth alone right now, but sleep tugs him under again. Only when something loud—a laugh, a gunshot—

shatters the oblivion, and alerts him to the world he's abandoned, does he resurface and open his eyes. In those brief clicks of consciousness, he sees Ruth—now wearing her glasses, pushing the channel button on the remote control as it were a morphine pump. Sometimes he sees the television screen—dancing M&M's, the ravaged face of a middle-aged rock star, a bloody dagger, BBQ sauce being painted on ribs, an SUV climbing a staircase, a map of Bonanza burning, a cat dancing the cha-cha, the basset-eyed newscaster, green shapes rolling over a weather map, a comely woman eating worms, their empty co-op lobby, commemorative president portrait plates, a man's face going through a window, a planet exploding. And sometimes, just as sleep gets hold of him again, just as he sinks back into tranquil nothingness, he sees Dorothy in the examining room, crouched on the linoleum floor, waiting for him to call her.

RUTH PAUSES AT THE NEWS STATION ON HER third go around. In the time it's taken Alex to fall asleep, a graphic for tonight's top story has already been designed—a long shot of the tunnel as seen by the night-vision bomb robot, and a bold red-and-black sans-serif typeface emblazoned diagonally across it, *Danger in the Tunnel.* She switches back to the BBQ sauce being painted on ribs, to the gold-edged dinner plate bearing Ronald Reagan's face, to their lobby as seen by the security camera near the vestibule door—a skinny boy of twenty, their upstairs neighbor who always forgets to take off his wooden clogs, strides through the lobby on his way out.

When Ruth had cast her vote against the camera, she did it with galling righteousness, warning her neighbors, too young to remember, about giving up their privacy for false security. But once the system was up and running and their lobby played twenty-four hours a day on channel seventy-one, she had found herself tuning in from time to time, absorbed by the activity, oddly soothed by the steady bustle of life entering and exiting their building. When Alex had asked her what could be so engrossing about watching their neighbors come and go, she said, "Remember Mrs. Birukov sitting on the stoop all day long? We were so sure she was spying on us, that she was the FBI's informant in the building. Maybe she was just an old woman who found solace in the hubbub."

When the front door closes behind the skinny boy, the long, narrow black-and-white lobby looks, to Ruth, no more or less foreboding than the long, narrow phosphorous green tunnel playing on all the other channels. Compared to the fate of one little dog, nothing else matters.

How can he sleep at a time like this?

How could she not? Fatigue pervades her every cell. The whirligig of imagery exhausts her. Whatever they might face tomorrow, rest will only help. She mutes the sound and goes to the medicine cabinet. All three shelves are overflowing. Alex's prescriptions dominate the top one, hers the middle, Dorothy's the bottom. She scours her shelf for her over-the-counter sleeping pills, a foil-backed, plastic sheet of eight perforated squares, each square holding a little blue diamond of sleep in its own air bubble. She finds the sheet, but the diamonds are gone. She must have swallowed the last one yesterday evening. She fingers through the rest of her shelf—expired penicillin, Lipitor, hemorrhoid cream, Advil, Aleve, Excedrin Migraine, an ancient jar of skin lotion, ear plugs—for some alternative (any label that warns of sleepiness). She checks Alex's shelf—Gas-X, Zantac, Nexium, Cystex, Sudafed, Proscar, Viagra, Avapro, Toprol, hydrocortisone, and one disintegrating roll of antacid chalk. She even searches Dorothy's—Zubrin, Soloxine, heartworm pills, Advantage, chicken-flavored toothpaste, Atopica, Clomicalm, and a vial of sedatives for travel.

She can't be up all night, not tonight. She'll descend

into a vortex of panic and worries far more disturbing than anything she saw on television. She and Alex have to be up, showered, and dressed before Lily arrives. The young couple she's bringing over might overlook the five flights of stairs, the water stain on the ceiling, but they'll certainly take notice of a septuagenarian couple greeting them in their bathrobes.

She reaches for Dorothy's vial of travel sedatives and reads the label: *one quarter tablet for dogs up to eleven pounds one half hour before traveling, or when needed.* She tries to do the arithmetic. How many times does Dorothy's weight go into hers? Her mind goes blank. She struggles with the childproof cap and pours two pills onto her palm. Placing them on her tongue (they taste like chicken), she turns on the faucet and drinks from the stream, like an animal. She half expects the very act of swallowing them to calm her, but she feels anything but quieted. She returns to the living room, covers Alex with a blanket, and shuts the lights. She mutes, but doesn't turn off, the television. It will act as a night lamp should he awaken in the dark.

She goes to their bedroom, changes into her nightgown, sets the alarm for seven, and puts it on her side of the bed. But she's hardly ready to lie down and close her eyes. The sedative's label instructed the dog's owner to allow the pills a full half hour to work. It's only been ten minutes.

She wakes up their computer, asleep on a tiny desk next to the bed. She opens the icon for their dial-up server, a connection so slow that it alone sometimes puts her to sleep. When the search engine comes up, she types into its thin window, *dog dachshund herniated disc.* Six hundred and eight matches appear. She can't get herself to click on any of them. She stares through the electric blue lines of Web addresses, as if they were the slats of a Venetian blind.

Finally, she clicks the top link, a dachshund magazine. The cover features three dappled, shorthaired puppies about three months old, sunbathing near a swimming pool. Articles this month include *All You Need to Know About Disk Disease* and *Spring Finds Many Puppies Available*. She guides the cursor up to *All You Need to Know About Disk Disease*, but she can't yet make herself open that door. Behind that door are nerves and bone and blood. She rolls the cursor down to *Spring Finds Many Puppies Available*. Behind that door is youth and spring. She forces herself to click on *All You Need to Know About Disk Disease*.

> The spinal cord is protected by membranes called the meninges. The innermost layer, the pia, contains the highly vascular network that delivers nutrients and removes wastes from the nervous system. The meninges are inverted by numerous sensory nerve fibers called meningeal nerves. When a disk herniates into the spinal canal, the meningeal nerves become compressed and inflamed . . .

She stops reading: she already knows the article isn't going to divulge the only answer she needs. Is *Dorothy* going to be okay? On either side of the text, in the left-and right-hand margins, are advertisements—dachshund calendars, doxie dolls, hot dog bun beds, dachshund jewelry, doxie duds. There is also a dachshund adopt/rescue site and a dachshund memorial garden with a grief-counseling chat room and a link to buy pet sympathy cards.

Rainbow Bridge Cards
Design your own card
and send it to someone on the Net
who's lost a pet.

Below is an example: a white rabbit in a field of grass. The message: *My deepest sympathy for the loss of your rabbit.* Ruth bursts out laughing, covers her mouth so as not to wake Alex, and then remembers he's asleep in the living room. She scrolls down to the next example, a hamster in a wicker basket: *Losing a precious furchild is so difficult.* When she laughs this time, she suspects that the breathy explosions escaping from her throat are more hysteria than hilarity.

The next service offered by the Rainbow Bridge Company is personalized death notices. *In Memoriam* the card line is called. The example: a black-and-white studio portrait of an Irish setter with today's date, January 9, 2004, and an inscription that reads: *It is a sad day in our lives. Joey "Oggy" Richards, our best friend, and our son, died of heart failure. Marty and Mary Richards.*

Ruth quits, signs off, clicks on Sleep. If only sleep were that easy. She climbs into bed, but she still isn't drowsy, despite the sedatives and the fatigue pooled in her limbs. She reaches for the book on her night table, *The Portable Chekhov*. When she first retired, she read every new novel praised by the *Times,* a languid pleasure nearly impossible while she was busy teaching, but lately, she's can only bear the company of long-dead Russians.

The table of contents includes: *At Christmas Time, An Attack of Nerves, Heartache, A Calamity, The Man in a Shell, The Lady With the Pet Dog*. She opens to *The Lady With the Pet Dog,* an old favorite.

A new person, it was said, had appeared on the esplanade; a lady with a pet dog. Dmitry Dmitrich Gurov, who had spent a fortnight at Yalta and had got used to the place, had also begun to take an interest in new arrivals. As he sat in Vernet's confectionery shop, he saw, walking on the esplanade, a fair-haired young woman of medium height, wearing a beret; a white Pomeranian was trotting behind her.

And afterwards he met her in the public garden and in the square several times a day. She walked alone, always wearing the same beret and always with the white dog; no one knew who she was and everyone called her simply "the lady with the pet dog."

"If she is here alone without her husband or friends," Gurov reflected, "it wouldn't be a bad thing to make her acquaintance."

The first thing Ruth notices is that the little dog, which she had remembered as vital to the story, isn't nearly as important as she imagined. The Pomeranian is only a prop—an excuse really—for Chekhov to get the lovers to meet.

He beckoned invitingly to the Pomeranian, and when the dog approached him, shook his finger at it. The Pomeranian growled: Gurov threatened it again.

The lady glanced at him and at once dropped her eyes.

"He doesn't bite," she said and blushed.

"May I give him a bone?"

After their first tryst, before either is aware of the profound love awaiting them, "the lady with the pet dog" sits dejected on the hotel bed, weeping with remorse, while Gurov, a little bored and impatient, cuts a slice of watermelon and eats it "without haste," Ruth's favorite line in the story. She would try to get her tenth graders, mostly teenagers from the Jacob Riis projects, who had never been in love, though some of the girls were pregnant, and who didn't know where Russia was, never mind Yalta, to understand the perfection of that detail, the promise of transformative love implied in the callous act of enjoying a watermelon slice while the woman you've just made love with cries. Chekhov doesn't mention the Pomeranian in this scene, but Ruth knows the little dog must be somewhere in his mistress's hotel room bearing witness.

She can hear sirens on First Avenue; a helicopter passes overhead. She looks down again, but she can no longer focus. Who can concentrate on a slice of watermelon with everything that's going on?

ALEX SURFACES. THE LIVING ROOM'S ONLY light source is the muted television. Ruth has covered him with a blanket. He rises from the sofa to look for her. It's not until he locates Ruth—wherever he wakes up, whatever the hour—that he feels oriented.

She's asleep in their bed, supine, breathing evenly, her face empty of worry. The reading lamp is shining. Her glasses rest askew on her nose. Her *Portable Chekhov* lies tented on her chest. He has loved her for so long that he can no longer distinguish between passion and familiarity. He slips off her glasses, puts away her book, douses the light, and returns to the living room. The windows face north, in the direction of the tunnel. If ten thousand gallons of gasoline had exploded, surely he'd see a red glow. The night sky is as monochromatic as always.

He goes to his studio, the back bedroom facing the airshaft, and switches on the lamp over his worktable. He never approaches his unfinished tome, especially in the middle of the night, without wonder and fear. Wonder that it's still alive; fear that, with the next mark, he will kill it.

Sending away for their FBI files had been Ruth's idea. When the Freedom of Information Act declassified the cold war documents in the late nineties, all their old lefty friends, even those who had traded in their manifestos for the Torah, had sent away for theirs. You couldn't dine at someone's house without the files coming out, if they weren't already on display, next to the photo album. The length of the dossier was a point of pride, the bigger the better, a vita of activism, proof that the wizened hostess, who had to use a magnifying glass to read about her glory days, had once been a tigress. "Nine hundred and six pages," she would tell her guests. "What a waste of taxpayers' money. A school could have been built for what it cost to spy on me. Who knew I was so important?"

When his and Ruth's files finally arrived, three years after they sent for them, he could see that Ruth was a little disappointed by the page count. "How could Bernice"—the wizened hostess—"merit over nine hundred pages when all she did was sign a few petitions?" Ruth had said, and he understood. Didn't he feel the same way when a less deserving artist rated a bigger review?

At first, he and Ruth read the files as if they were entries in a journal they'd forgotten they'd kept: *Cohen, Alex (b. 1928), New York City. Honorable Discharge from the army, 1946. Cohen née Kushner, Ruth (b. 1930). Graduated City College, 1952. Subjects married on April 22, 1953. Arrested November 15, 1954, disobeying court order: marching without a permit: Citizens Against the H-Bomb. November 26, 1955, at 1:55 p.m., informant observed subject, Ruth Cohen, entering a teacher's union meeting. On May 6, 1956, confidential informant of known reliability, turned over to the NYC*

Office, The Nation, with information that the subject, Alex Cohen, was illustrating for the Communist organ. Informant told NYC Office, that subject, Ruth Cohen, assigned Anton Chekhov, a known Russian writer, to high school students.

When they finished the book on them, they reread it, this time trying to ferret out from the scant clues, who, exactly had betrayed them. "October 12, 1967, neighbor was interviewed telephonically. She was most cooperative and expressed great admiration for the FBI. She told agent that subjects' trash pail contained remnants of a banner for *The Lower East Side Women Against the Vietnam War.*" Which neighbor? Mrs. Birukov, the old Ukrainian who practically lived on the stoop?

Ruth eventually tired of the intrigue and went back to reading fiction, but not Alex. The beauty of the pages had captivated him. The sheets came blackened out, or partially obscured, the names of informants shrouded. What remained was sheer abstraction, the very shapes of subterfuge, the silhouettes of duplicity. The idea of illustrating the actual files came to him months later in a used-book shop. He saw a copy of the *Book of Hours* and knew instantly how he'd utilize those pages. In place of crosses and saints, martyrs, and angels, he'd paint A-bombs, Mouseketeers, two-tone refrigerators, Khrushchev, and portraits of him and Ruth. Instead of ornate, delicate gold-leaf borders, he'd stencil on the perforated patterns of vintage nineteen-fifties paper doilies. Instead of the Bible's Psalms, he'd copy the FBI's accusations.

Alex sits down at his worktable, a door on two saw-horses. All he needs to complete page fifty-one is a Prussian blue line around the edge, and a final pattern of cardinal red stenciled over the chrome green borders. He searches his worktable for just the right doily to use as the pattern, one with a little geometry, but all he finds are flower designs. Daisies aren't what this composition needs. He'll have to cut a stencil himself. He reaches for his X-Acto knife and a thin piece of cardboard. Holding the knife like a pen, he carves a perfect triangle, about the size of a sequin, in the board. He then stabs the freed shape with the knife's point, and gently excises it. He repeats this cut thirty more times and thirty more specks are excised. His vision begins blurring, but he won't allow himself to look away. If he looks away, he'll break the laser point of concentration drilling out each design, and his attention will scatter.

Everywhere.

It will include not only the knifepoint, but also his old fingers gripping the knife's silver waist. It will take in not only the manuscript page he is finishing, but all six hundred and ninety-nine pages still waiting to be illuminated, and his studio filled with a lifetime of work in the terrified city on the panicked island by the nervous continent.

In such a wide worldview, Alex fears his ebbing hope that art might make a difference and Ruth's crumbling belief that a difference can still be made, will surely get lost, and then what will they be left with?

A sick little dog.

ALARMS BLARE. HUMANS RUN PAST EVERY which way. The nearest one, a male nurse, springs open the cage next to Dorothy's and reaches inside. Still wrapped in a yellow towel, eyes milky, tongue lolling, the Chihuahua is carried past Dorothy's cell and laid on a steel table. The nurse begins banging the creature's lifeless ribs with his fist. "Get Doctor Griffon, fast," he shouts to another nurse, a female, who is trying to calm the other restless dogs stacked in cages.

Despite the liquid tranquility dripping into Dorothy's neck from the plastic cloud overhead, she is nervous, too. She knows the male nurse isn't going to rouse the Chihuahua, no matter how hard he beats it, and that the female nurse isn't going to convince the other caged animals that Death isn't in the room.

Dorothy is not staying here. She looks for a way out. If she can just get her front claws under a wire or two, she might be able to loosen them and squeeze through. But her claws never catch a wire. Her nails barely scratch the surface. She is so weakened by pain and paralysis that all she manages is to feebly swat at the bars, like an old cat.

"Where do you think you're going, little mama?"

Dorothy freezes. She doesn't whimper. She doesn't raise her eyes to see who or what is speaking. She keeps her head down, her posture small and submissive. If she doesn't look up, maybe Death will forget about her and choose another?

Death unlatches her cage and reaches for *her* this time. Dorothy bares her little yellow teeth at Death. When he doesn't take her seriously, she snaps at him.

"I'm not going to hurt you," Death says. His mustachioed face fills her open cage door as he reads the plastic hospital tag around her neck. "I bet they call you Dottie, don't they mama?"

Death knows her name.

She snarls again and Death quickly steps back this time. Dorothy doesn't let down her guard though. She's seen birds fly into windows, a rat die of poison, the remains of a deer on the parkway. Dorothy suspects she isn't going to stave off Death with a mere show of teeth.

Death returns with a muzzle. He will win any contest of strength. She changes her strategy. When he tries to muzzle her, she licks his fingers.

"Okay, mama, you don't have to wear it."

He slips a surprisingly warm hand under her and carries her and the liquid cloud out of the cage. He holds her tight and high against his chest, like she is his own baby. From that angle, Dorothy sees the Chihuahua still being pummeled by a fist. Death ferries Dorothy down a long, brightly lit corridor into a small, dark room with a huge machine. Death's assistant, a female nurse, is waiting for them.

"How's the Chihuahua doing?" she asks.

"Don't ask," Death says. He strokes Dorothy's head; she's trembling. "You want me to shave her?"

"Let her relax a minute." She takes Dorothy from him. "You allergic to anything, precious?" she asks before reading Dorothy's chart. "Strawberries! Coconuts!"

"No more piña coladas for you, little mama," Death says.

Another of his assistants, a female anesthesiologist, peers around the door. "Are we ready?"

"The radiologist isn't in yet," the nurse says.

"Prep her. I'll be right back."

The nurse hands Dorothy back to Death, takes out a silver tray, and begins to set out bottles and cotton balls and what look, to Dorothy, like knives and forks and spoons.

The anesthesiologist shoulders open the door without using her hands this time and the nurse helps her put on rubber gloves. The rubber gloves reach for Dorothy. "What's your name?" she asks.

"Dorothy," Death says.

"Dorothy, you're going to feel very sleepy in a minute." She lays Dorothy on a table while Death prepares a syringe. "Start with twenty ccs. Let's see how she does."

Death injects the plastic tube connecting Dorothy to the cloud, and tranquility saturates her. She sinks and rises at the same time. One minute the cloud is above her, the next below her.

"It's almost seven-fifteen for God's sake. Find out where the hell Doctor Whitehead is," the anesthesiologist tells the nurse.

"I'm right here," a man says, pushing open the door while simultaneously shedding his camel hair coat. The nurse hands him a white one. "Traffic was a nightmare. I was out in Long Island visiting my mother, she going to be eighty next week. The Midtown's still closed. The BQE is a parking lot. Then some moron cop pulls me over to do a spot security check. Trucks are speeding by hauling God knows how many tons of explosives, and he pulls over a Porsche. I'll be back in a second."

The instant the door closes behind him, Death says, "Best son in the world, risks terrorists and fights traffic to visit his old mother. Five to one, he's banging that horse lady in the Hamptons again."

"You still with us, Dorothy?" the anesthesiologist asks. She pries open one of Dorothy's eyelids with her rubber fingers. "Let's give her another ten ccs."

And Death willingly complies.

Saturday Morning

THE INVASION

ALEX AND RUTH DON'T NEED THE ALARM clock to wake up this morning. They're up with the first flush of dawn. Their bedroom window faces east to a stand of black chimneys in a field of tar roofs. The view hasn't changed since the day they moved in. Today, the roofs are wet with snow. Without yet knowing the other is awake, they each silently watch the sun scale the brick parapets and silhouette the chimneys in gold. This same view of sun rising over rooftops has been as fundamental to Alex's understanding of color as any sky by El Greco. He has studied it during monochrome winters, varnished with spring rain, feverish from summer colds, in the throes of passion, when his life felt insufferable or heady with promise, as he and Ruth went through every season of marriage.

For Ruth, the spectacle of sunrise is less inspiring than comforting. The rise of the sun is like the opening of a novel she's read so many times that she can take pleasure in the details and nuances without having to race to the end to find out what happens. She watches as the sun finally clears the chimneys, igniting the snow into blinding copper. For an eyeblink, their window, curtains, ceiling and walls, her folded eyeglasses on the nightstand, all turn apocalyptic red. Then the fiery radiance abruptly dies, as if someone's thrown water on the young sun, and a pale wintry orb ascends over the rooftops.

Alex's cheek is creased from sleep, his upended white hair a wave about to crash. Ruth's eyes are jelly and bloodshot from the sedatives. Steam whistles in the pipes. Footfalls resound on the ceiling. A car alarm goes off. Everything is so ordinary that their hesitation to rise and face the upcoming day feels unreal. Then Dorothy's absence in their bed hits them.

"Do you think she's had the test by now?" Ruth asks.

"It's too early," Alex says. He checks the time anyway, only to find that Ruth has moved their clock, with its magnified numbers, to her side of the bed. He can see she's set the alarm for seven, when Dorothy's test is to be performed. The clock's minute hand is narrowing toward the appointed hour, but Ruth doesn't seem aware of the impending alarm. She's still staring out the window. He reaches over her and defuses the ringer.

"What if the test tells us nothing?" she asks. "Do we go ahead with surgery? Shouldn't she have every chance?"

"Let's wait to hear what the doctor says. Maybe it's good news."

Ruth reaches for her glasses; Alex inserts his hearing aids.

They each swing their legs over their respective bedsides. To face the intrepid buyers Lily is bringing over at eight-thirty, Ruth puts on a new housedress, a cardigan, wool socks, and loafers. Alex finds a fresh white shirt and a pair of clean slacks. Ruth runs a brush lightly over her thinning gray halo; Alex slicks down his white stalks with a wet comb. Ruth starts the coffeemaker; Alex turns on the news.

Last night's graphic—the truck's headlamps as seen by the night-vision robot with *Danger in the Tunnel* splashed across it—appears on the screen. The morning newscaster, the blond in Washington, D.C., promises that after the station break she'll be right back with an exclusive interview with the truck driver's family and friends.

"Maybe they caught him and it's over," Alex says.

"It's not over or they would have changed the graphics," Ruth says.

She goes back to the kitchen. A minute later, one fifth of the way through the block of commercials, a delectable scent that Alex can't quite place distracts him and he follows it. Ruth is standing over a boiling pot on the stove, using the right burner because the left's knob is missing. At the bottom of the pot, amid the dancing bubbles, is a single stick of cinnamon.

"Lily said it would make the place smell homier." Ruth's face is pink from the steam, her glasses streaked and opaque. "Why doesn't the doctor call?"

The truck driver's uncle and mother have faces like walnuts, shiny tacks for eyes. They're standing on a snowy sidewalk before a row house in Queens. Behind them, neighbors jockey for a position on the television screen. The mother wears a massive black garment under an overcoat and a headscarf, though Alex and Ruth can't tell if the scarf is worn for warmth or for religious conviction. It looks like something their grandmothers might have worn. The uncle, a stout man with a black mustache as big as a pocket comb, reads a statement in a stiff guttural accent that goes slack with emotion: "Abdul Pamir is a devout, gentle, and caring son, husband, father, uncle, brother, and nephew. He was born in Uzbekistan, and became a proud American two years ago. We want him to come home safely."

A snapshot of Pamir, smiling in a Mets baseball cap, appears in the upper-left-hand corner of the television. He can't be older than thirty. He has beautiful teeth.

The uncle escorts the mother back into the row house, but not before the reporter, a redheaded man in an orange parka, attempts a question, "Do you think he'll turn himself in?" The mother silences him with an outstretched hand, a root ball of fingers, and closes the door.

The interviewer turns to a neighbor who has been waiting patiently, at military attention, for his chance to speak. "He's a good man," the neighbor intones into the microphone, "he helped me fix my toilet."

The phone rings. Ruth grabs the extension on the coffee table, while Alex mutes the set.

"Dorothy's holding her own. She made it through the myelogram without complications," Dr. Rush tells her. "Unfortunately, the test indicates that the rupture is worse than we hoped, disc material is pressing directly against the cord. Her best chance now is immediate surgery."

"She needs the operation," Ruth tells Alex.

"Ask if she'll be able to walk again?" Alex says.

"If we go ahead, will she walk?"

"I don't know."

"He doesn't know," she tells Alex.

"Ask what her chances are?"

"Can you give us odds?" Ruth asks.

"Seventy-thirty, but it's only a guess."

"In her favor?"

"I'm afraid not."

"Thirty percent," Ruth tells Alex.

"Of pulling through or walking?"

"Walking," Ruth says.

"Ask what her chances are without the surgery."

"If we decide not to?" Ruth asks the doctor.

"Miracles happen, but that's what it'll be, a miracle."

"It will be a miracle," Ruth tells Alex, then cups her hand over the phone. "What should we do? I can't lose her, Alex. I'm not counting on miracles."

"Are we doing this for Dorothy?"

"She's under sedation," Dr. Rush prompts. "The longer she's under, the more stress on her heart."

"Are you sure?" Alex asks Ruth.

"Yes," Ruth says. "Yes," she tells the doctor, "go ahead."

Dr. Rush hangs up, but Ruth doesn't let go of the receiver. She still has more questions. "Should I have asked if the surgery had other complications?"

"Maybe it's better we don't know," Alex says.

The buzzer sounds at eight-thirty sharp.

"Will you let Lily in? I need a moment to myself." But as soon as Ruth says it, she finds she can't bear to be alone. She follows Alex to the front door, and while he attends to the intercom and buzzer, she unlocks their apartment, though Lily has a key.

"Are you inside?" she shouts down the stairwell.

Three sets of footsteps start up. Ruth can tell already that the climbers aren't used to such a steep ascent. They're expending all their energy on the first flight and not conserving any for the fifth. What if Dorothy can't walk? Have they done the right thing?

A lanky young man clad in leather and his even taller wife, breathtakingly beautiful with enough black hair to stuff a pillow, trot up the last steps. They're not even winded, but Lily is. She huffs up behind them. She's almost Ruth's age with a figure like a gym sock stuffed with tennis balls. Her red hair sports white roots, but she always wears a fresh coating of crimson lipstick. She's been selling walk-ups in the East Village since mid-century, but recently, she confided to Ruth, the stairs have become too much for her, too, and she doubts she'll be able to make the transition to the new elevator condos springing up on every corner. The management companies don't want to deal with an old battle-ax like her.

"Where's your little dog?" she asks when Dorothy doesn't appear as usual, barking at the top of the stairs.

"She's having surgery," Ruth says.

"Oh, my," Lily says.

The lanky young man, the black mane, Lily holding an armful of open house fliers, Ruth and Alex walk Indian-file through the narrow doorway into the apartment. Ruth can't help but take note of the couple's first reactions: his icy appraisal of the living room's length and breadth, its ceiling height; her restrained but evident distaste for their decor—the Ikea bookcases, the blond Danish coffee table, their plaid sofa that was the rage in the seventies, and the muted, glowing TV. A map of Uzbekistan flickers on the screen: Pakistan, Kazakhstan, Kyrgyzstan, Turkmenistan, and Afghanistan flank its borders, one -*stan* amid many. The couple wanders toward the kitchen.

"Turn off the news," Lily whispers to Ruth and Alex as she passes by, then calls after the young couple. "You have to wear sunglasses to eat breakfast in there."

Lily's waving hand catches Alex's attention; she's motioning the couple into his studio. He hurries down the hall after them. He can't leave his work unattended, unprotected.

"It's a good size for a guest bedroom and there's plenty of light with the air shaft," Lily says.

Thumbnail sketches on paper napkins, pictures torn from magazines and newspapers, Polaroid snapshots, small pieces of canvas are stapled, tacked, or taped to every wall; paint-smudged doilies dry on chair backs; Xeroxed memos, all bearing the FBI's seal, are piled on the floor; paintings choke the remaining space.

"It could be a nursery someday," Lily says.

Alex watches the young couple's faces as they struggle to imagine the room—a madman's cell—cleared of his history.

Lily leads them into his and Ruth's bedroom. "There's nothing obstructing the view, you wake up to sunshine," she says, parting the curtain to reveal the tar roofs.

Alex can see by the couple's disappointment that the chimneys won't be a daily lesson in color, but an eyesore. They open the closet—his ten-year-old tartan robe hangs from a hook, Ruth's favorite housedress, with the missing button, droops beside it.

The entourage heads toward the bathroom, but Alex

doesn't follow. He and Ruth scrubbed every tile in preparation for today. They bought a new shower curtain and even scoured the grout around the tub with bleach and Q-tips.

"Only one bathroom?" he hears the young man ask.

"Yes, but it has a window," Lily quickly points out.

Alex finds Ruth. She's waiting by the bedroom phone. Dorothy's been in surgery for almost an hour. Before the couple leaves, they thank him and Ruth for giving them a first look. Lily follows them into the hall, closing the door behind her.

"Do you think that went well?" Ruth asks.

"There's good news and bad," Lily tells them. "They like the apartment, and they *love* the neighborhood, but they're worried about the tunnel, like the rest of us. Is there any news?"

Alex turns on the television: Live Press Conference pulses in the screen's upper corner. Camera lights, as bright as competing suns, irradiate a makeshift stage in the lobby at city hall. A burly man, captioned *FBI Spokesman,* the short mayor, and the buzz-cut police chief in full regalia approach a lectern crowned by microphones. The burly spokesman reads a statement: "At eight twenty-two, the aqua-bomb detector finished its sweep of the tank. As of this hour, we believe there is no bomb." Barrages of questions are hailed at him, but he ignores them. "We're asking New Yorkers to stay on high alert until the driver's in custody." The mayor leans into the microphones. "Keep your eyes and ears open, but go about your lives. Soon as the city engineers give the go-ahead, mine will be the first car through the tunnel. We will not take questions at this time."

The screen bisects into halves—the basset-eyed newscaster in New York and the blond in Washington.

"What they're not saying," the blond says, "is that Pamir might be wearing the bomb and that's why they didn't find one in the truck."

"You're right, Kat, the device could be on him and he could be anywhere at this point."

The buzzer sounds. Ruth jumps. Not because she thought she heard a bomb go off, but because for a split second, it sounded like the phone had rung.

The next couple, two middle-aged women, one tall and dour, one short and dreamy, have brought their dog, a boisterous adolescent labrador.

"It turns out there's no bomb!" Lily greets them at the top of the stairs. "Isn't that wonderful!"

"They caught Pamir?" the tall one asks.

"Not yet," Lily says.

Tugging on the lead, exhilarated from the cold, heady from the climb, intoxicated by the new smells, the labrador rushes past Lily into the apartment.

"What's your dog's name?" Ruth asks.

"Harold."

Harold spots Dorothy's rubber mailman and lunges toward it. It takes everything in Ruth's power not to grab the lead and stop him. Once Harold has the mailman in his jaws, though, he loses interest in him; the mailman might as well be a piece of old gum. Harold spits him out and spots the tennis ball. He bolts forward, chomps down on it, drops it, rolls it with his nose, and chases it into the kitchen.

"I guess Harold wants to see the kitchen first," Lily jokes.

In hot pursuit, Harold skids across the tiles and then abruptly freezes. Something of greater urgency has caught his attention. Lead by his nose, he searches for it. He sniffs under the counters, around the table legs, the garbage pail, the refrigerator, Dorothy's bowls, but it's not there. He zig-zags across the kitchen floor until he finds it. Ruth recognizes the spot. It's where Dorothy lost control of her bladder.

"You have to wear sunglasses to eat breakfast in here," Lily says.

The phone finally rings. They excuse themselves to take the call in the bedroom. Alex shuts the door, while Ruth answers the phone.

"Dorothy's out of surgery. She's being moved to recovery now," Dr. Rush tells her. "She's breathing on her own and all her vitals look normal, but as we were closing her, she had a seizure. We're not sure what caused it and we're not sure if the seizure will have lasting effects. We'll just have to wait and see."

"What kind of effects?" Ruth asks.

"The anesthesia should start to wear off in the next few hours. She'll either come out of it or not."

Someone raps on the door. Alex opens it: Lily, the two women, and Harold fill the hall.

"Could they see the bedroom before they leave?" Lily asks.

Alex widens the door. The two women peer in. Ruth hangs up. She sits stiffly on the bed's edge, cast in cold Vermeer window light, her stare lost on something outside the picture frame. The women realize they've interrupted a moment of grave privacy and withdraw, but not Harold. If it weren't for the grip on his lead, he would fly onto the bed with Ruth.

"Dorothy had a seizure," she tells Alex, as soon as they're alone. "She may or may not wake up."

"When will they know?"

"When the anesthesia wears off."

"Did the surgery go all right?"

The stoic forbearing in Ruth's veneer cracks. She looks at Alex as if he'd asked her his name and she couldn't remember it. "I forgot to ask."

Alex picks up the phone, dials the hospital, and asks for Dr. Rush.

"May I take your number?" the nurse says.

"My wife just spoke to him."

"He's attending to an emergency," she says.

"He's calling back?" Ruth asks.

"After his break," Alex says.

This time of year, at nine-thirty on the dot, the sun disappears behind the new twelve-story elevator building on the corner and, for seven minutes, their bedroom becomes a cave.

Ruth remains on the mattress's edge; Alex joins her. She's more shadow than mass. They don't speak. What is there to say? When the sun finally reappears, it's like a second sunrise.

They stand once again and open the door. While they were holed up in their cave, the apartment has been invaded. A woman wanders down the hall counting electrical outlets. A little boy stands at one end, flicking the light switch on and off. In the kitchen, a middle-aged couple, florid-faced and breathing hard from the climb, are helping themselves to glasses of water. Lily fields their questions as best she can. "The co-op has no plans to put in an elevator." "There *is* a washing machine and dryer; it's in the basement."

Others arrive: a man wanting to know if their apartment is wired for high-speed (Alex doesn't even know what that means); a woman wondering if she can keep plants on the fire escape because where she now lives, they don't allow plants on the fire escapes, and she's adamant about growing her own tomatoes for medical reasons; the couple upset about the pigeons in the air shaft. "Are they permanent?" they ask Lily. "I don't think they're migratory," she says.

Another assault ensues: the pianist trying to calculate if the century-old floor joists can bear the weight of his baby grand, never mind that it won't fit through the door; two men curious to know if the co-op would prevent them from tearing down the kitchen wall to open up the space; the horse-faced woman in sweatpants and yellow rubbers asking if the co-op would allow her to see clients, though she never once mentions what she does; the harried couple in matching red parkas who never take off their hoods. She strides around the apartment, while he watches the news on his cell phone.

"Have they found Pamir?" Alex asks.

The hood shakes no.

"We have a million-dollar decision to make," the other hood says. "Turn off the goddamn news."

Alex and Ruth slip back into their bedroom to try Dr. Rush again, but a young woman in high-heel boots is sitting on their bed. "Would you mind if I lie down for a sec? I'll take off my shoes. I want to see what the view looks like from here."

Ruth is appalled, but Alex shrugs.

The woman unzips her knee-high boots, places them next to Ruth's slippers, and stretches out on the mattress; she doesn't get up for ten minutes. Then a man leaves the window open in Alex's studio, and they and Lily have to rush around gathering up all the FBI memos and sketches blowing across the floor.

Finally, the window's shut; the art is picked up; the woman's risen from their bed. Ruth dials the hospital, while Alex shuts the bedroom door.

"Dr. Rush was supposed to call us back," Ruth tells the recovery room nurse.

"He's still attending to the emergency," she says.

Why didn't Alex tell her? She braces herself for the worse. "How's Dorothy?"

"Sleeping. We're trying to wake her every fifteen minutes, but she hasn't yet responded. We'll keep trying."

Someone taps on the door. Alex answers it. "Excuse me," says a man sporting glasses thicker than Ruth's, "but do you know where I could buy a replacement knob for the stove?"

. . .

"I think it went very well," Lily tells them as she gathers up the leftover fliers in the living room. She's showing another apartment at one and is running late. "The two ladies and Harold are interested, and the couple in the matching parkas asked about the building's finances, but I doubt anyone's going to make a firm offer as long as Pamir's out there. Let's hope they catch him soon. Good luck with your little dog." She closes the door behind her. A small lake remains in the hall from the runoff of so many dripping boots.

DOROTHY'S EYELID IS PRIED OPEN. A WAND OF light pierces her sleep. "Time to get up, little mama."

"Try rolling her."

A force stronger than gravity shovels her over.

"No response. Should I call Rush?"

"He's still on duty? Where's the surgeon?"

"Gone back to the Hamptons. The horse lady called. I took the message. I guess he wants to be the second car through the tunnel, after the mayor's."

"She's got to be thirsty. Wet her lips and see if you can get her to lick them."

Until the drops of water are painted on her lips, Dorothy doesn't even know she's thirsty. Now all she craves is to slake her cruel thirst. She licks Death's sweet-tasting fingers.

"Don't give her too much."

His fingers withdraw, but not before the restorative water has worked its miracle. Dorothy opens her eyes and releases a high-pitched sigh of such gratitude that even Death, who's heading out the door to find Dr. Rush, turns around.

"Welcome back, Dorothy."

Saturday Afternoon

THE WAR

ALEX GOES TO SAHARA'S FOR TAKEOUT, WHILE Ruth carries the mop and pail back into the kitchen, then airs out the rooms. The horse-faced lady had smoked in the bathroom; the tomato-lady had been doused in noxious perfume; even Harold's lingering smell is offensive. She wants these alien odors out of her house. While the windows are open and the rooms chilly with drafts, she sits before of the glow of the television set, as one sits before a fire on a cold afternoon.

The basset-eyed newscaster looks as exhausted as Ruth feels. He's interviewing a pretty woman with bad teeth. They face each other in comfortable wingback chairs. A red, white, and blue lightshow plays on the gigantic plasma screen behind them. The caption reads, *Hostage in Her Own Home.* "We have an exclusive with Debbie Twitchell, the twenty-six-year-old bartender who spent two harrowing hours with Pamir yesterday evening. Twitchell lives in a basement apartment in Midtown, less than four blocks from the tunnel's entrance."

The camera closes in on Debbie's face; she looks as if she's been holding her breath the whole time the newscaster spoke; she looks like she's going to explode if she doesn't get her story out, now. "I was very scared. I knew something was wrong when I saw him on the stairs. Please don't hurt me, I say. He says, If you don't scream I won't hurt you. He has an accent but it never dawns on me he's a terrorist. I don't know what Muslim sounds like. He pushes me inside and looks to see no one else is home. I think for sure he's going to rape me, but instead, he asks me to turn on the TV."

"Did he show any anger at this point?"

"No, he wants me to switch to the news. The thing about the tunnel and the suicide bomber is on; I can see him get fidgety. He's sweating and he won't take off his coat. I start to put two and two together; he must have a bomb under the coat."

The basset-eyed newscaster looks directly at Ruth and anyone else watching. "What Pamir does next will shock you. We're talking with Debbie Twitchell, hostage in her own home."

"He says, What kind of pills do you keep in this house? I say, What kind do you want?"

"You say that?"

"He has a bomb. I don't want to die. I didn't know terrorists take drugs. He forces me into the bathroom and makes me get in the tub. He's looking everywhere for my pills."

"Does he find anything he wants?"

"All I have are antidepressants. He's getting really jittery. He keeps asking if I have anything stronger. I keep thinking he's going to press the button on his bomb."

"Did you see the bomb?"

"No, like I say, he keeps his coat on. He says he's going to kill me if I'm lying. I think maybe if I do everything he asks, he'll let me live. So I say I have some crystal meth."

Ruth isn't sure she heard Debbie right. The basset-eyed newscaster isn't sure he did either. "You offered Pamir methamphetamine? A man you believe has a bomb under his coat?"

"Soon as I say it, I think, what have you done, Debbie? You're going to give a terrorist the thing that made you crash your car and steal from your mama. I think you've just killed yourself. But I try to stay cool. I say, Have you ever done ice? He says he hasn't. He wants me to show him how to do it. I make him two lines. I say, Here you go. He says, Aren't you going to do it with me? I didn't want to, I've been clean for three months. I only keep a little bit in the house as a test from God. But I don't want to die either. So I do a quarter of a line."

"And he does the rest?"

"Yes. I ask him if he minds if I pray. I don't know if God will even listen to my prayers because I'm high. He says no, so I ask him if he wants to pray with me."

"Did Pamir pray?"

"I think so. He mumbles something in Muslim, then jumps up and runs out the door. God heard me even though I was high."

Alex and Mr. Rahim watch the interview on a small set shelved in a corner of Sahara's. Alex sits on a counter stool, while Rahim stands over a vat of boiling oil, waiting for Ruth and Alex's falafels to bob to the surface. Without taking his eyes off the set, Mr. Rahim opens a fresh package of pita and tosses two onto the grill. He blindly reaches for a knife, and dices lettuce, tomato, and onions by feel alone. The falafels rise and gyrate in the bubbling heat. With tongs, he plucks out the sizzling balls and drops them into the hot bread pockets. He slathers hot sauce on Ruth's, tahini on Alex's, then wraps them in old-fashioned waxed paper.

"Who would give an intruder methamphetamine?" Alex asks.

"The stupid girl thinks Muslim is a language," Mr. Rahim says.

Tonight's polling question fills the screen: *Do you think terrorists take drugs?*

Alex pays, while Mr. Rahim settles the sandwiches in a paper bag and adds napkins and pepper, but remembers not to add salt. Alex can't have salt these days; he and Mr. Rahim often compare their high blood pressure medicines.

"Tell me, Alex," Mr. Rahim says, "do you think terrorists take drugs?"

Alex isn't sure if he's joking or not.

Mr. Rahim smiles. "I know if I was going to blow myself up, I'd definitely take something." He slides the bag over to Alex. "My prayers are with your little dog."

At the bottom of their staircase, Alex pauses to look up. It's like climbing to the top of a lighthouse. He only takes two steps at a time when Ruth's around, though if asked, he'd deny it. But today, even if she were cheering him on, he couldn't sprint up. Between last night and this morning, he can barely make it to the third landing without using the handrail. The oxygen seems to be thinning as he ascends. He stops to let his heart slow down when he sees Ruth's face hanging over the rail.

"Dorothy's opened her eyes, Alex! She's taken water!"

Ruth pours them each a glass of wine in celebration of Dorothy's turn for the better, while Alex sits down. The kitchen table is already set with silverware and cloth napkins. She arranges the falafel sandwiches on plates, and then throws away the bag, but not before salvaging the paper napkins and pepper. She squirrels those away in a drawer already crammed with enough take-out napkins and free pepper to outlast them both. The television is off. After the hospital called, she didn't want the news droning in the background.

"Drinking water must mean she's fighting," Alex says, biting into his sandwich.

Ruth has no appetite. Only now is it dawning on her that she forgot to ask, yet again, how successful, or not, Dorothy's operation was. Maybe she doesn't want to know the answer?

"Dorothy's telling us she wants to live, Ruth."

The phone rings. Alex answers, while Ruth braces for what she's sure is coming next: the nurse taking back the good news.

He shakes his head in wonder. "Harold's Ladies have made an offer," he tells her.

"With Pamir still on the loose?" She picks up the cordless extension. "Did they catch him, Lily?"

"I don't know any more than you do," she says.

"How much?" Alex asks.

"Eight hundred and fifty thousand."

"So low?" Ruth says.

"They're gambling on you and Alex panicking and selling while you think you still can. Let's face it, if Pamir turns out to be a suicide bomber, prices could drop even lower. What should I tell them?"

Ruth and Alex exchange looks. "It might be our only chance to sell," she says.

"Maybe we should take it."

"What if Pamir turns out *not* to be a suicide bomber? If we sell now, and everything returns to normal, we'll have priced ourselves out of the city, let alone an elevator building. I'm scared, Alex. What if he turns out to *be* a suicide bomber? We might not get another offer for months, maybe years."

"What would you do?" they ask Lily.

"Stall. But not for too long."

They finish their lunch in front of the television. A press conference is taking place on City Hall's steps. Behind a thicket of microphones, the mayor solemnly lowers his head and waits for the dozens of reporters to grow pin-drop silent. When he finally looks up, his expression is that of a father about to tell his children there's no money for Christmas.

"If it's bad news," Ruth says, "maybe we should grab the offer."

"If it's bad news, there might not be an offer."

"I just got off the phone with Baltimore's police chief,"

says the mayor. "Twelve minutes ago, an oil tanker truck collided with oncoming traffic and overturned on the Francis Scott Key Bridge. Eight people were killed, three others are in critical condition, including the driver, who remains trapped in the vehicle."

"Does the mayor think the two incidents are connected?"

"Is the driver wearing an explosive device?"

"Do you think it's a new pattern of attack? Is the second driver from the Middle East? When can the police question him?"

"When I have answers, you'll have answers," the mayor says.

The phone rings.

"What if we waited too long, Alex? What if they're taking back their offer?"

"What if it's the hospital?" he says, reaching for his extension. She picks up hers.

"We have a bidding war!" Lily tells them. "The Red Parkas just made a counteroffer, eight hundred and seventy-five."

"How can that be?" Ruth asks.

"Are you watching the news?" Alex asks.

"It's what we realtors back in the nineties used to call the Mugging Principle. Someone's mugged on your block and all the neighbors want to sell. Prices drop. But if muggings start happening on every block, regardless of neighborhood, then muggings no longer factor into the market price. If everywhere is equally dangerous, even Baltimore, you might as well live in New York. I put a call in to Harold's Ladies."

The Francis Scott Key Bridge now spans their screen: dead center, the tanker lies on its side. Its neck appears broken. The tractor cab, with the driver still inside, is dangling over the railing by a cable that looks, to Alex and Ruth, no thicker than a horse's tail.

Even before the phone finishes its first ring, they grab their respective extensions.

"Harold's Ladies are willing to go up to eight eighty," Lily says, "but you have to decide now. They don't want to get into a bidding war. They were emphatic about that, said the offer's good for five minutes only." Lily pauses. "Should I pretend I couldn't reach you and call the Parkas?"

"Where would we be? Who would go out today?" Ruth asks.

"They asked about your little dog. I could tell them you went to the animal hospital."

"They must know we have a cell phone."

"Don't animal hospitals forbid cell phones? Human ones do"

"I guess it wouldn't hurt to say we're at the hospital."

"Call the Parkas," Alex says.

Fire trucks, bomb squad vans, hovering helicopters, ambulances, squad cars, bulldozers, all bejeweled by whirling red lights, begin rolling across the bridge toward the truck.

The screen splits in two. The results of this afternoon's poll appear on the right:

Do you think terrorists take drugs?
78% yes
20% no
2% not sure
with a margin error of 3%

The phone rings.

"Good news or bad? What would you like to hear first?" Lily asks them.

"Good," Ruth says.

"Bad," Alex says.

"Harold's Ladies are threatening to drop out, and the Parkas haven't returned my call yet."

"What's the good news?" Ruth asks.

"A third party has entered the fray, the lady with the horsy face. You remember, she was wearing yellow rubbers and sweatpants."

"I don't remember any yellow galoshes," Alex says.

"She talked about seeing clients of some sort. Do you think the co-op would object?"

"Depends what kind of clients," Ruth says.

"How much?" Alex asks.

"Eight eighty-five."

"Should we take it?" Ruth asks.

"It's hard to say. These days, once a bidding war starts, everyone loses reason. I've had couples practically offer their firstborn. Last week two got into a preemptive battle; the apartment wasn't yet listed. But this isn't your usual war. Let me do this: I'll inform Harold's Ladies and the Parkas about the new offer. All they can say is no. Meanwhile, I'll call Yellow Rubbers and tell her you're still at the animal hospital, incommunicado."

While they wait for Lily to call back, Ruth switches to another news channel. This one is also broadcasting the spectacle of emergency vehicles, red lights whirling, rolling across the Francis Scott Key Bridge toward the truck with the broken neck. She tries a third news channel, but the rescue pageant is all that's playing. Station by station, she keeps searching for the breaking story that will help her make the right decision. She holds the remote at arm's length, like a pistol, and fires—bridge, rescue pageant, tanker truck, dangling cab, bridge again. Her arm grows weary, but she doesn't lower her aim. The phone finally rings again. She grabs it with her free hand, beating Alex to the draw. "What did the Parkas say?"

"Eight eighty-six. They're bid surfing, trying to ride the crest of the big round numbers."

"Harold's Ladies?" Alex asks on the extension.

"They'll only make another offer if we switch to a sealed auction. They want the final bids opened at their lawyer's office. They want an end in sight. My guess is they'll offer nine even."

"What about Yellow Rubbers?" Ruth asks.

"She's willing to go along with whatever you decide."

Alex tries to decipher from Ruth's frazzled, obstinate, confused expression if she's made a decision any more than he has. Her hair is so thin these days, a puff of white smoke around the noble outline of her skull. The muted television's light plays over her face like refracted water. He can see her thinking, her gray irises swimming back and forth across the fishbowls of her glasses. He's looked into those fishbowls for over half a century: there's not one secret left. He knows the forces at war in Ruth's features, the frown of righteousness and the knit brows of pragmatism. He counts on Ruth to guide them. Even if the needle on her moral compass is spinning wildly, Ruth will find her way.

He hears his wife—whose ethics has been his bedrock and his muse and his shackles, who wouldn't lie about her beliefs to the House Un-American Activities Committee even when it cost them friends, passports, his first retrospective, almost her beloved teaching job—say to Lily, "Tell all of them we're still at the hospital and see how high Yellow Rubbers will go."

"I don't know if I'm wishing that it's just a horrible coincidence and Baltimore is safe," Ruth says to Alex as they wait for Lily to call back, "or if I'm hoping the truck is rigged to explode so that the Mugging Principle will hold and we'll be able to afford an elevator. Who would wish for such a thing? Who would make up such a principle? *If everywhere is dangerous, prices go up?* There must be a couple just like us in Baltimore who are watching TV, praying that what their realtor told them is true: as long as Pamir's on the loose in New York, Baltimore's market won't crash. A plague must be visited upon both houses and then, only maybe, we can afford to stay in our neighborhood? I fought my whole life for peace and now I'm wishing Baltimore blows up so that we don't have to change pharmacies? My God," she says, shaking her head in surprise and self-disgust. "Old age robs you of every last illusion, even the belief in your own goodness. What's next? Will I be wishing for gasoline trucks to start capsizing in Los Angeles or Miami so that we can move to Sutton Place and have a doorman?"

Ruth studies Alex, sitting beside her on the sofa, to see if he agrees, though she's not exactly sure what she wants him to concur with—that there's a couple just like them in Baltimore or that it's okay to wish a bomb on them? She puts her hand on his thigh. She can feel the muscle tighten and jump; his feet start tapping. They're always tapping, his unstoppable feet and his tireless legs, legs that never give up, ready to climb not just the five flights of stairs but the whole ladder to heaven, two rungs at a time. Whenever she needs to feel that force, she touches his thigh.

"I don't give a good goddamn about goodness. Would it be so bad to have an elevator *and* a doorman?" he says at last. "Don't we finally deserve some peace?"

DOROTHY AWAKENS IN HER CAGE. DEATH IS nowhere in sight. She feels as if she's been cut in two, and then stapled back together. To her left, strung with tubes, lies the faintly breathing Chihuahua, and to her right, garroted in an Elizabethan collar, lies the Pomeranian, his eye packed in blood-soaked cotton.

A face, cratered as the moon, appears above Dorothy. "So you finally woke up, little hot dog," says the doctor with the kind blue eyes.

He opens her cage and reaches inside, but he doesn't pick her up. He cups her numb back feet in his warm hands instead. She senses him trying to squeeze life back into them; she feels pressure, though she's not sure if the pressure is in her feet or in her desire to please. He checks her incision, running the length of her back, and then prods the base of her spine. His fingers patiently knead her tail. The pressure returns, though this time, the warm pads of his fingers spark her tail to life. She can feel the tip rousing itself.

"Dorothy, are you trying to wag your tail? Can you wag it again? Come on, little hot dog, wag your tail. You can do it, yes you can. Wag your tail. Give me one little wag."

Dorothy senses him finally give up. He starts to close the cage door. She doesn't want him to go. She can't be alone with the faint breathing and the blood-soaked eye. She musters every ounce of strength and will, obstinacy and faith, and manages to thump her tail once, loudly, against the bars.

AT THE TOP OF THE NEWS HOUR, FOUR O'CLOCK sharp, the phones on the coffee table begin chiming again. Ruth mutes the television and reaches for her extension, but Alex stops her.

"Lily will call back," he says. "I'm not sure of anything anymore, Ruth. Should we sell? Stay? Flee? Do terrorists take drugs? But as flummoxed as I am, one thing I know for certain. Lily will call back. It's time to figure out what *we* want."

Ruth feels as lost as a penny in a well.

"The silent auction is off," he says. "Why the secrecy? Do we want to go to Harold's Ladies' lawyer's office Monday morning, and practically have heart attacks as he opens each of the sealed bids and announces our fate? Once they're opened, Ruth, there is no turning back. And this bid surfing must stop. Enough. The Parkas' shenanigans are going to drive away any serious buyers. From now on, we only accept bids in increments of five thousand. And as far as the co-op approving of Yellow Rubbers seeing her clients in the apartment, how many clients do you imagine are willing to climb five flights of stairs, I don't care what kind of services she performs."

"I agree, no silent auction," Ruth says. "It's humiliating to have the bids opened at their lawyer's office, to treat us like dishonest children. How do we know they won't switch the envelopes? But the bid surfing is keeping things alive. Harold's Ladies, the Parkas, Yellow Rubbers, they must be as anxious about the news as we are. They must be nervous wrecks, jumping every time the phone rings. Let them jump. Let the phones ring. Let fatigue set in. Anything but quiet. If it's too quiet, they'll be able to think. If they think, they'll change their minds. You were right all along, Alex. *Who would buy an apartment this weekend?*"

The phones start up again.

"I'll tell Lily," she says, picking up her extension. "Hello."

"Dorothy's wagged her tail," Dr. Rush tells her.

"Dorothy's not paralyzed! She'll be able to walk?"

Alex grabs his extension. "That's such good news!"

"Yes, it's very good news, but I have to caution you, we've seen no movement in her back legs."

"You mean," asks Ruth though she knows perfectly well what the doctor means, "Dorothy will be able to wag her tail but not walk?"

"We don't know. We just have to wait and see."

"Is she in any pain?" Alex asks.

"We're making her as comfortable as we can. I'll call if there's any change."

Cradling the receiver, Ruth says, "At least she'll be able to wag her tail and let us know if she's happy or not."

Alex aims the remote at the television and clicks volume, but Ruth steps into his line of fire. "She made it through the surgery and now she's *wagged* her tail. Let's take some pleasure in that. I need a break."

She takes the remote out of his hand, replaces it with his wineglass from lunch, picks up her own, empty save for a drop of Merlot, and clinks rims.

"To Dorothy," she says, and then defiantly throws back her head until the ruby of wine rolls down her glass's mouth into her open lips. It's a gesture Alex knows so well; she's been using it to celebrate victories for as long as he can remember.

Ruth puts down her glass and settles beside him on the sofa. They hold each other.

At this hour, when the sun first dips below the western rooftops, their living room has an especially soft light. The windows, as far as he and Ruth know, are the originals. The panes were already as yellow as old paper and as scratched as old eyeglasses when they moved in. When the late-afternoon sun enters the room, the ancient glass acts as a filter to diffuse the harshness of the horizontal rays until the room and everything in it looks covered in white powder.

When the phone next rings—the bedroom extension, the cordless in Alex's studio, the original olive green wall mount in the kitchen, and the two on the coffee table before them—the light appears to shatter.

"I tried calling earlier," Lily tells them, "but there was no answer and then your line was busy. Harold's Ladies need an answer by five. They called the animal hospital and found out that visiting hours are over at four-thirty."

"You can tell them now," Alex says. "We don't want a silent auction."

"Are you sure? Are you watching the news? Baltimore is

a false alarm. Witnesses say a seagull flew into the truck driver's windshield. He's in the hospital. No bombs."

"Isn't that good news?" Ruth asks.

"For Baltimore," Lily says.

"Are we sure about our decision?" Ruth asks, as soon as they hang up.

"Nothing's changed," Alex says. "All that's happened is a bird flew into a windshield and everyone panicked."

"You're wrong, Alex," Ruth says. "I changed. I couldn't wait to take advantage of Baltimore's troubles. When an accident there affects real estate here, when a dead seagull can elicit such terror in us, everything's changed."

The phone rings again.

"I'm sorry to call back so soon, but Harold's Ladies left another message on my cell," Lily says. "They're offering nine hundred and fifteen until five on the dot."

"Tell them you couldn't reach us," Alex says. "Tell them we already left the hospital. Tell them we never turned our cell back on. Tell them we're old and forgetful. Tell them anything. We're taking the night off."

Saturday Evening

CEASEFIRE

ALEX AND RUTH HAVE A DATE TO DINE THIS evening with Rudolph and May, their oldest friends as well as Alex's gallery dealers. The two couples meet every other Saturday, usually at one of the coffin-narrow, ten-table ethnic restaurants in the neighborhood. They always arrive just as the kitchen opens, six sharp. If they dine any later, the loud, ebullient crowd takes over, and Alex and Rudolph, despite twelve thousand dollars' worth of hearing aids between them, can't make out a word of what's being said.

Rudolph is tall and concave with features that look chipped from flint. May is as flat and thin as a popsicle stick with a gloriously thick gray braid worn down her back. Now seventy-six, the braid finally reaches the base of her spine. Despite May's family's wealth, bluebloods from Boston, she always looks shabby, whereas Rudolph, a ragpicker's son, dresses like a count.

Rudolph and Alex grew up together in Washington Heights, two bright, ambitious immigrants' sons seeking entry into New York's culture. Where Alex's talent was for painting, Rudolph's acumen was for marrying May and then parlaying her respectable inheritance into a vulgar fortune. In the early fifties, when Rudolph could finally afford to buy his own gentility, he opened a gallery. His first exhibition was Alex's war paintings, canvases Alex had worked on since his discharge, battles of color composed on stretched, army-green canvas tents. Rudolph came up with the exhibit's title, *Drawing Fire*. For being Alex's first and most steadfast patron, Rudolph has earned Ruth's loyalty and love.

May, on the other hand, was more problematic for Ruth. When the men first introduced them, Ruth knew she had to make this friendship work. She wore her best dress from Macy's, polished her teacher's pumps, and sported her new red cat-eye glasses, while May showed up in an old powder-blue cardigan from Bonwit Teller and tennis shorts. A thin but icy frost blanketed their exchanges for decades until Dorothy came along. When Ruth saw May get down on her hands and knees to address the new puppy at eye level, she finally understood that those regal manners, which she thought feigned, were genuine and extended to animals: May spoke to Dorothy as an equal.

Tonight at dinner, a decision must be made. Ruth and Alex plan to ask May and Rudolph for their help finding a small museum, or even a foundation, where Alex can donate his older work. They can't continue to store it when they move. Resolving what to do with Alex's unsold work fills Ruth with relief, whereas it fills him with anxiety.

They turn up Second Avenue in search of Xza-Xzu's, a new restaurant May read about in the *Times*. Ruth has no memory of what cuisine Xza-Xzu's serves. She isn't even sure which continent she and Alex are headed to. She studies the faces of passersby to see if anyone else is troubled by the possibility that Pamir might be lurking among them, but no one seems to care. The shops are full, the bars packed. They find Xza-Xzu's shoehorned between a Polish diner and a Korean vegetable stand. When they open the door, incense and peppery spices sweeten the blast of heat. A little bell announces their arrival. The interior is as dark as a movie theater. Ruth can't see where she's going, though she can hear Rudolph's baritone greeting, and May's demure hello, coming from the back of the den. She follows the voices. Rudolph and May are wedged in a corner table, trying to read menus under a light no brighter than a dashboard's.

"Dorothy's in the hospital; she had back surgery," Ruth says, before she and Alex even take off their coats and sit down. Rudolph and May are, for lack of a better term, Dorothy's godparents. Should anything happen to her and Alex, Rudolph and May have promised to take Dorothy. They adore her and dote on her whenever she visits, to the disgust of their fifty-three-year-old son, a failed film producer, who still lives with them.

"Oh, no," May says. "Will she be all right?"

"Why didn't you call?" Rudolph says.

"We were sitting down to dinner last night. You know how Dorothy always gets to the table before us," Ruth says. "We found her in the kitchen, unable to walk. She couldn't even crawl away from her urine. When Alex picked her up, she shrieked. We used the cutting board as a stretcher. The tunnel had just been closed but no one knew why yet. It took us two hours to get to the hospital, then the guard wouldn't let us in because Dorothy's collar kept setting off the metal detector."

"They have metal detectors at an animal hospital?" Rudolph asks.

"All the signs look good," Alex says. "She made it through the surgery and wagged her tail."

Ruth can see May's eyes brighten with tears. She doesn't want to give her false hope. "The doctor cautioned us that wagging her tail doesn't necessarily mean she'll be able to walk."

"The doctor also told us that as long as Dorothy has one live wire running down her spine, there's hope," Alex says.

"He said if she feels *pain* there's hope," Ruth corrects him, though she knows how pointless and petty she sounds: when it comes to Dorothy, she wants the record straight.

"In either case, there's hope," May kindly intervenes.

A tall, slender waiter with Asian eyes, tobacco-brown skin, and dyed blond hair twisted into what look like corn stalks, hands Ruth and Alex menus. "If I can answer any questions," he says in a British accent.

"What kind of cuisine is Xza-Xzu's?" Rudolph asks.

"Pan-equatorial," the waiter says.

"Who has an appetite in such heat?"

"Would you like to start with a glass of palm wine? It's our house special."

"Bring us a bottle," Alex says, usually the least adventurous of the four when it comes to new tastes.

"It's been a long day," Ruth says. "Dorothy's surgery was at seven, and the open house started at eight-thirty."

"You had the open house?" Rudolph asks.

"People actually came?" May asks. "Were they aware of the tunnel?"

Rudolph turns to May. "Who didn't know about the tunnel?"

"They knew," Ruth says. "They came *because* of the tunnel. They were looking for a fire sale."

The waiter brings the palm wine and pours a splash into each of their glasses.

"It's sweet," May says, tasting hers.

"It's like Manischewitz mixed with coconut milk," Rudolph says.

"May I take your orders?" the waiter asks.

"What's not spicy?" Rudolph asks.

"What can be made without salt?" Alex asks.

"We can steam the Galápagos fish and put the sauce on the side."

"What kind of fish?" Rudolph asks.

"Wild salmon," the waiter says.

"Isn't salmon a cold-water fish?"

"I'll have the Tarawa chicken," May says, closing her menu.

"How many spices can they grow on Tarawa? It's an atoll. I'll have the same," Rudolph says. "Does it come with a salad?"

"Yes, and coconut rice."

"I'll have mine without dressing, please," May says. "And no rice."

"Pour it on mine," Rudolph says.

"Is there some other fish you can steam? I'm allergic to salmon," Alex says.

"We can steam a Papua perch."

"Does the sauce have salt?"

"It's equatorial cuisine. I believe everything has salt," the waiter says.

"Without the sauce," Alex says. "And just a little dressing on the salad."

Ruth orders the sampler plate, not out of curiosity, but because she can't bear to make another decision today.

"Did you get any nibbles on the apartment?" Rudolph asks as soon as the waiter leaves.

"We have a bidding war," Ruth says.

"That's marvelous!" May says.

Ruth shakes her head. "The first offers were so low we couldn't accept them. As long as Pamir is out there, we'll be lucky to get our asking price. You can't imagine our day. The phone didn't stop ringing. We never knew if it was the realtor or the doctor calling. It was touch-and-go with Dorothy for a while."

The waiter arrives with the salads; *all* the plates are swimming in oil.

"She asked for the dressing on the side," Rudolph says, as the glistening leaves are set before May.

"I asked for *light* dressing," Alex says. "And where's my wife's salad?"

"I didn't order one," Ruth says.

"I thought it came with the meal," Rudolph says.

"The sampler plate is an appetizer," the waiter explains. "It doesn't include a salad."

"Bring her a salad anyway," Rudolph says.

"With or without dressing?" the waiter asks, smiling at Ruth with such stilted politeness that it borders on contempt.

"I don't care," Ruth says.

Alex's feet start tapping as he waits for his lightly dressed salad to arrive. He dreads the conversation coming up. The fate of his unsold work stirs up such anguish.

"I have to ask," Rudolph says. "What kind of a person shops for an apartment during a red alert?"

Ruth begins. "This one girl, twenty, twenty-five at the most, asks if she can lie down in our bed."

"Under the covers?" Rudolph asks.

"If we weren't standing there, probably. She wants to see the view from our pillows. She agrees to take off her boots first."

"That was thoughtful of her," May says.

"She makes herself at home, sprawls across our mattress like a queen. She doesn't move for eight minutes. I checked my watch."

May and Rudolph laugh in horror.

"I need to do something with my old work," Alex blurts out.

The new salads arrive: May's is dry, Alex's is barely glazed, and Ruth's is an island of lettuce in a sea of dressing.

Under the table, Ruth settles her hand on Alex's knee to still his feet, but she receives a jolt of his anxiety instead.

"Alex," Rudolph says, starting right in on his salad. "You need to concentrate on the new work. May and I have a good feeling about this next show. These FBI pieces are timely. There's interest. Why confuse the old with the new?"

"Maybe he's right," Alex says to Ruth.

"We're selling our apartment tomorrow," Ruth reminds him.

"The collectors want high concept these days. We finally have an angle with your FBI pieces, Alex. Everyone's nostalgic for the Cold War. It reminds them of a time when the worst enemy imaginable was a gorgeous Russian spy in James Bond's bed, or Rocky and Bullwinkle's Boris and Natasha. Picture a Saturday-morning cartoon show about a squirrel and a moose and a cell of Jihadists?"

May drizzles an eyedropper of dressing on her salad. "Rudolph's right. People used to spend hours in the gallery studying the paintings, asking questions. Nowadays, they sweep in talking on their cell phones, and if they don't get the artist's intention between calls, they lose interest."

"This next show could put you back on the map," Rudolph says.

What map? Alex wasn't lost to begin with, Ruth thinks.

"It'll open up so many more opportunities," May adds.

"They'll be fighting to get your old work," Rudolph says.

Beneath the tablecloth, she can feel Alex's feet finally come to a rest: unlike her, he seems ready to drop the subject of his old work despite their agreement that the paintings can't move with them.

The waiter arrives with the dinners.

"We haven't even finished our salads," Rudolph says, annoyed. "Come back later."

"The dinners will only get cold," May says.

"Can you keep them warm in the kitchen?"

"They'll get dried out," May says. "Leave my chicken, please."

"Leave my fish," Alex says.

"Take mine back," Rudolph says. "I like my salad first."

"What are we supposed to do with all the paintings?" Ruth asks, turning to Alex. "Pack them up like the dishes? It's like moving a museum! We can't take care of them anymore, Alex. They need to find a home."

"What Rudolph meant," May says, motioning the waiter to leave, "is that we'll gladly store them at our warehouse until we figure out what's best."

"That's what I said," Rudolph says. He finishes his salad and then samples May's chicken. "It tastes like lemongrass and KFC." He looks for the waiter.

"I told you not to send back your dinner," May says.

As they wait for the waiter to return with Rudolph's dinner, Ruth stares down at her sampler plate, aching to thank May for her kindness, but she knows that if she does, she'll only embarrass the men. Their friendship depends on the unspoken agreement that the gulf between their finances, even in the guise of free storage, is never openly acknowledged.

Alex stares down at his fish and rice, now as appetizing to him as rocks and sand. Nothing is really resolved. He can't shake the feeling that once his old canvases are warehoused, they'll be forgotten, even by him. Their conception once mattered to him as much as his own life. While he painted, the battles he experienceed were as intense as any in the war—sometimes more so. In his studio, he was both the hero and the enemy.

"Did either of you catch the interview with Pamir's hostage?" May asks.

"Terrorists don't take drugs," Rudolph says, looking around for his dinner. "If they took drugs, they wouldn't need to be terrorists."

"Don't let Rudolph fool you, he's as scared as the rest of us," May says. "He keeps an inflatable kayak in the guest bedroom in case of a dirty bomb. The plan is for the three of us to portage it to the Hudson, assemble it amid crowds running amok, and then paddle to New Jersey, flinging off those who try to cling to our stern."

"May scoffs but when I bought it, she was the one who insisted on a watertight compartment to carry ample supplies of iodide pills and canned food."

"If you're going to build a bomb shelter, you might as well stock it," May says.

Rudolph's dinner finally arrives.

"The plate is *very* hot," cautions the waiter.

The sauce, pudding-thick, is bubbling, but Rudolph takes a bite of his chicken anyway. He chases it with ice water. "You need nuclear fission to get food that hot," he says.

"All the more reason to have an ample supply of iodide pills," May says. She turns to Ruth and Alex. "Have you found a place yet?"

"We just started looking," Ruth says. "Everything is so expensive."

"You should get the hell out of here while you can," Rudolph says.

"Maybe the stairs are a blessing, at least they're forcing you to make a decision," May says. "We talk about leaving all the time. Move the gallery to Santa Fe. But our son despises Santa Fe, so we do nothing about it. You know what a weekend like this does to us? Nothing. Rudolph checks to make sure the kayak's inflated and all I feel is lassitude. I'm like a gazelle caught in a lion's jaw—limp, numb, resigned to my fate. Our son thinks the only reason Osama hasn't struck again is because he has the Hollywood syndrome. Now that he's had an extravaganza, he's not going to settle for a small, artful, independent feature."

"Before we all run off to the South Seas, remember, this is the dreck we'll be eating," Rudolph says, spearing the last of his chicken, and then pushing away his empty plate.

"It is awful, isn't it," May says, setting down her cutlery. She's barely touched her food.

Alex's perch is long gone and Ruth's dinner is just crumbs now, though she has no memory of what anything tasted like.

Rudolph reaches for his fork and begins picking at May's untouched chicken. "Didn't you say that the *Times* gave it a good review?"

The waiter appears. "Would you like to hear about our desserts? Tonight we have fried mango sorbet with guava syrup and cheesecake."

"They make cheesecake on the equator?" Rudolph asks.

"I believe our cheesecake comes from Passaic, New Jersey."

"The check, please," May says, quietly handing the waiter her credit card as he leaves.

"We'll pay the tip," Alex announces.

"I wouldn't tip this guy," Rudolph says.

"Is Dorothy allowed visitors?" May turns to Ruth. "We forgot to ask."

On the street, the two couples hug good-bye.

"You'll call us about Dorothy?" May says.

"Thank you for everything," Ruth whispers.

"Next time dinner's on us," Alex announces.

"Let me know when you want the paintings moved," Rudolph says.

"Good luck tomorrow," May adds.

Ruth, a head shorter than May, and Alex, almost two heads shorter than Rudolph, watch their friends start west toward Fifth Avenue, the waist-length braid swinging behind them.

"I know she was only trying to be kind," Ruth says. "But how could anyone imagine that facing five flights of stairs at our age is a blessing?"

"I'm not sure the warehouse is such a good idea," Alex says.

They turn and head east toward the projects.

The temperature has risen: the air feels almost balmy. Ruth unknots her scarf, undoes the top button on her overcoat: she's always the hotter of the two. Alex puts on his red baseball cap. It's a little after eight, early by East Village standards. The Saturday-night crowd isn't even awake yet. The dominatrix haute-couture shop, the trance music store, the drug paraphernalia stand are all empty. Tompkins Square, lit by old-fashioned arc lamps, looks especially inviting. Ruth takes Alex's arm and they enter the park. The snow on the path has already melted, but above them, in the latticework of elm branches, whiteness abounds. It's a white Alex would mix with Chremnitz white and a touch of hansa yellow.

When Ruth looks up, it's not the snow she notices; it's the black pieces of night between the white branches. At this time of year, the sky usually looks as low and gray as a tin ceiling, but tonight, it looks exactly like what it is—infinite.

On warm winter Saturday evenings, the park's normally overrun with suburban teenagers, blasting music and skateboarding, but tonight, the only other souls are the elderly Italian couple who run the cheese and ravioli shop and the homeless chess player who frequents the library on cold days. He and Ruth have discussed books. He, too, is fond of the dead Russians.

"It's so quiet," he says to no one in particular.

"Maybe they should close the tunnel permanently," the Italian husband says.

"Maybe they should close all the bridges and tunnels and leave us our island," his wife says.

Alex and Ruth exit the park and cross the street to the newsstand. They barely glance at the evening headlines, *No Bomb in Baltimore.* It's the classifieds they want. Ruth pays, while Alex hoists up the voluminous *Sunday Times*, clamps it under his arm, and, like a schoolboy carrying a schoolgirl's heavy books, walks her home, all the way up the mountain of steps.

The phone machine has no new messages. Ruth isn't sure if she's relieved (the hospital didn't call, Dorothy must be holding her own) or disappointed (no one has made another offer). Alex turns on the news, while she sits at the kitchen table to scout the real estate pages, a section thicker than the international news, for a two-bedroom elevator co-op below Fourteenth Street. She takes a pen from her purse to circle any possibilities. Out of the thirty-three two-bedroom open houses taking place downtown tomorrow only one is listed for under a million dollars.

Junior 2 Bedroom
Great for students or first-time buyers
Needs TLC
Price Reduced!
$900,000

What is there to do but circle it? She searches the next tier of prices.

Dazzling Sun-Filled Corner Two Bedroom
Built-in Bookcases!
Window Seat Soaks Up Morning Sunshine
$1,100,000

She not only circles this one, but draws a big star beside it. It's higher than they wanted to go, but . . .

"Any news?" she shouts over the television.

"The mayor just gave another press conference. He wants New Yorkers to call the hotlines *only* if they have a credible sighting. The FBI has received over ten thousand calls. Did you find anything?" he shouts back.

"Someplace that sounds too good to be true. Do you

think all the sightings will affect prices? Don't prices go up if everywhere is dangerous? Or does the market stay flat if sightings happen in all the neighborhoods? Do you remember what Lily said?"

Alex comes into the kitchen and peers over her shoulder. She's drawn a big black star next to one of the listings. He knows that to draw a star that black on paper as absorbent as newsprint, she must have pressed very hard on her pen. He reads the fine print: *One million and one hundred thousand.*

"We can't afford it," he says.

"We can if we learn from Harold's Ladies. If we like the apartment, let's offer a hundred and fifty thousand less than the asking price, two hundred less if the news is still bad tomorrow morning. If we don't take advantage of the panic, someone else will. What's the worst that can happen? The sellers will laugh in our faces? We laughed at Harold's Ladies, and look at us now." She puts down her pen. "My God, I almost wished for bad news. Do you know what the worst that can happen is?"

"We'll have to put off moving for a few months?"

"That my wish will come true."

In bed, after she sets the alarm for seven, Ruth reaches for her *Portable Chekhov* and opens to the page that she'd been reading last night when she fell asleep. The lady with the pet dog is crying once again, though in a different hotel, many years later. This time rather than eat a slice of watermelon, Gurov takes her in his arms and experiences such compassion "for this life, still so warm and lovely, but probably already about to begin to fade and wither like his own. Why did she love him so much?" The lovers take council and try to figure out a way to spend more time together without secrecy and deception, despite living in two different cities, and his having a wife and a daughter and a job at the bank, and her having a husband and a Pomeranian, if the little dog is still alive.

Ruth already knows the lovers' fate—she taught the story almost every year—yet every time she nears the story's end, Chekhov creates anew the hope that this time things will turn out differently, this time "the solution would be found, and then a new and glorious life would begin: and it was clear to both of them that the end was still far off, and that what was to be most complicated and difficult for them was only just beginning."

Sunday

QUEEN FOR A DAY

DOROTHY NOW SHARES A SEMIPRIVATE ROOM
with a bulldog recuperating from having eaten a penny, a
poodle passing kidney stones, a Mexican hairless with a
sinus infection, and a pug in a leg cast. Cages line the
green walls. Dorothy's is stacked atop the bulldog's—she
can smell him trying to pass the penny. Unlike intensive
care with only the Chihuahua's faint breath for company,
this ward is alive with barking. Whenever the nurse walks
by, all the dogs vie for her attention, but Dorothy knows a
trick the others don't. As the nurse passes her cage,
Dorothy wags her tail to beat the band. "Look at you," the
nurse invariably stops and says, "twenty-four hours out of
back surgery and doing the shimmy. You go, girl, shake
that booty."

This morning though, a medical student with clammy
hands accompanies the nurse. He takes Dorothy from her
cage and sits her on a cold steel examining table.

When she wags her tail for him, he's not impressed. She
looks up at the nurse.

"I'm sorry, sweetie, you have to try to walk today."

The nurse helps her up, supporting Dorothy's hindquarters, while the medical student walks to the head of the table and calls, "Dorothy!"

Once again, she wags her tail for him—faster, harder—but wagging her tail doesn't even elicit a smile.

The nurse gently sets her down. "I'll be right back." She shouts into the corridor, "Mauricio, give me a little sausage from your McMuffin." When she returns she's holding what to Dorothy's nose smells like life itself. Dorothy hasn't eaten in thirty-six hours. Her entire world narrows to that smoky meaty scent. The sausage is passed from the nurse's long black fingers to the student's pale ones.

"Try calling her now," the nurse says.

The pale fingers hold out the crumble of sausage. "Dorothy!"

With the nurse's help, she's able to get traction on the table surface: she takes a step, sways.

"One more, baby, one more," the nurse whispers encouragingly.

Dorothy lurches toward the enticing morsel. She doesn't quite reach it, but she manages two more steps.

"I'm going to get Dr. Rush," says the medical student.

He leaves with the sausage. Where is he taking it?

"Aren't you something," the nurse says, "I bet you'll be ready to go dancing by tonight."

The doctor with the kind blue eyes comes in. Dorothy can smell he now has the sausage. "A hot dog eating a sausage? Sounds a little like cannibalism to me." He tilts up her snout and shines a pinprick of sun into her eyes. He cups a cold steel bell to her heart and listens. Dorothy follows the traces of meat in the air: the sausage is in his left hand. Finally, he offers her the morsel, but he holds it just out of reach. She rises to her feet again, this time without the nurse's help, takes a step, sways, takes another, totters, but keeps going until she reaches the meat.

"You are a miracle wiener," the doctor says, feeding her the last of the crumbles. She swallows them before she remembers to chew. All that's left to savor is the juice on the doctor's fingers. She licks up every last drop, and when the taste is gone, she washes his fingers in gratitude.

"GOOD MORNING, EVERYBODY," SAYS THE basset-eyed newscaster—freshly shaved, powdered, and clad in a new shirt and tie. To unshaven Alex and barely awake Ruth drinking their morning tea in front of the television, he looks as if he'd slept like a baby. "Before I bring on my first guest, a forensic psychologist and consultant for Homeland Security, to help answer the question—*Is Pamir a suicide bomber or not?*—let's see what the American people think. Here's how our viewers responded to this morning's polling question. Seventy-seven percent say yes, Pamir is a suicide bomber, twelve percent say no, and eleven percent isn't sure. We'll be right back to see if the experts agree."

"Nothing's new," Alex says.

"At least my wish didn't come true," Ruth says, answering the phone before he's even aware it's ringing. From his end of the sofa, he studies her expression, trying to decipher who's calling so early on a Sunday morning. She closes her eyes as if to listen with great concentration. When she opens them, her fishbowls are brimming with joy.

"Dorothy's walking!"

"Our girl's going to be okay?"

"She took five steps!"

He reaches for Ruth's free hand, squeezes. "When can she come home?" he asks.

"Not until tomorrow morning, but we can visit her after eleven today. Thank you, thank you, thank you," she says to the doctor. Alex watches her gently settle the phone back in its cradle as if she were putting it down for a nap. "Dr. Rush said it took a bribe of sausage to get her to take the five steps."

"Imagine if he'd have offered her pâté."

"He said she'll have to be confined to her crate for two weeks, but after that, we need to encourage her to walk."

"Two weeks of breakfast in bed; we may never get her up."

"The doctor called her a miracle wiener."

While Alex showers, Ruth leaves the television on, though she's no longer watching. She's stocking her purse with provisions for the day—cell phone, keys, the folded newspaper sheet with the open house addresses, paper and pen to take notes, and Dorothy's squeaky hot dog. The doctor said they could bring one of her toys. The plan is for them to look at the two downtown apartments—the junior two-bedroom in need of TLC and the one they can't afford—before catching the bus to the hospital. When the phone next rings, it's almost time to leave. She picks up the bedroom extension hoping Lily's calling with news from the bidding war front.

"So what's going on with this madman loose in New York?" asks her younger sister, Thelma.

In stereo, Ruth hears Thelma's television blasting the news in Fort Myers, and her own blasting the news in the living room. She closes the bedroom door. "We know nothing more than you do," she says.

Three years ago, Thelma retired from the post office in Queens and moved south with her new boyfriend, Teddy, to a senior community, Camelot Gardens. "It has two pools, a clubhouse with a media room, and when the time comes, assisted living, and it's all pet-friendly," Thelma had told her. Ruth has yet to visit. She loves her sister, but she can't bear Teddy, and Dorothy despises Thelma's two teacup Yorkies, Happy and Muffin. After their parents died, the sisters had little in common, except their love for their dogs. When Ruth and Thelma discuss their dogs, all the intimacy is back.

"We had such a scare with Dorothy, but she's going to be fine," Ruth says. "I just got off the phone with her doctor."

"Oh, thank God," Thelma says. "What happened?"

"Her back went out. She had to have emergency surgery. We didn't know if she'd ever walk again, but she's already taken five steps. Her doctor called her a miracle wiener."

"There's a woman in my Scrabble group who has a dog with three legs and she's says the dog gets around beautifully. When can Dorothy come home?"

"Tomorrow."

"Are you and Alex still going through with the open house?"

"We had it yesterday."

"You let strangers into your home with a suicide bomber running loose?"

"I doubt if he's house hunting."

"So, did you get any offers?"

"We think so, but it's so far below our asking price, we're not sure if we should take it."

"How much?"

"Nine hundred thousand."

"Oh my God, you're rich!" Thelma screams.

Muffin and Happy start barking.

"You know it buys nothing here," Ruth says.

"Move to Camelot Gardens. With your money, you could afford a Lavender Court Villa; it's top of the line. I haven't been inside one, but they all have pool views and granite countertops. And there's an arts and crafts room in the clubhouse where Alex can set up an easel."

"Alex needs his privacy to work."

"Hell, with your money, buy two units and let him paint in one. You'd live like a queen."

After the sisters say good-bye, Ruth can't help but wonder if she and Alex should reconsider Florida. Not Camelot Gardens of course, but somewhere near—though not too near—her sister. She tries to imagine her and Alex in Fort Myers, clad in their dark New York clothes, and Dorothy with her bad back, crossing six lanes of traffic and then miles of sun-blistering parking lots just to have a bite out or to pick up some milk and bread.

Alex fills his overcoat pockets with his provisions for the day—cash, wallet, antacids, allergy pills, extra hearing aid batteries, a comb, and Stim-U-Dents, while Ruth gathers up her gloves and scarf. Before walking out the door, they check the television one last time for the very latest news on Pamir, lest their path cross with his this morning.

"It's a big myth that suicide bombers are raving lunatics," says a double-chinned woman with badly applied lipstick captioned "Forensic Psychology Professor and Consultant for Homeland Security." "Anyone can become a suicide bomber. This is normal psychology, normal group dynamics. Normal people, given the right circumstances or the right set of friends can become suicide bombers."

"Is she telling us it's peer pressure?" Ruth asks.

"She's telling us that they haven't a clue where Pamir is."

HALFWAY DOWN THE BLOCK, ALEX BECOMES aware of sounds he hasn't heard in years—his own footfalls in slush, singing from the Pentecostal Church, a flock of pigeons taking off, voices of passersby, and distant sirens. He doesn't entirely trust his hearing aids, but to his old soldier's battle-alert ears, the sirens sound like a full barrage. "Do you hear them?" he asks Ruth.

"What?"

"Sirens."

"No more than yesterday." She takes his arm; the brisk air feels so good on her cheeks and throat; she's so happy they're not in Florida. "Doesn't knowing we're looking for the three of us make all the difference in the world? Wouldn't it be something if the junior two-bedroom turns out to be nice? It would almost be an even trade if we take Yellow Rubbers' offer. We'd even make a little profit if Harold's Ladies came through. And it's so close by: we wouldn't have to change pharmacies."

The building is a nondescript six-story box near the corner of Avenue C and Second Street. Ruth takes note of the façade—faux brick, graffiti, only two casement windows per floor, no windowsills, no stoop. The front door is unpainted steel.

She reads the directory next to the intercom. It doesn't bode well for the co-op's stability. Names have been crossed out, scratched out, and written over, a pentimento of transient identities. Open House is printed on a paper scrap taped beside 2G.

She hesitates before ringing.

"We're here already, Ruth. We might as well look."

She presses the bell, while Alex positions himself against the door to push as soon as the lock-release buzzer sounds.

The intercom crackles unintelligibly. The buzzer is louder than a truck horn. The steel door vibrates as if it were about to explode: Alex shoulders it open.

"We're inside," Ruth shouts back at the intercom. The lobby is big, but she's appalled at the color, Pepto-Bismol pink. The elevator smells of cigarettes. A low, thrumming rock-and-roll bass line greets her when the elevator opens on the second floor, despite it being nine o'clock on a Sunday morning. She squares her shoulders and knocks on 2G.

A tall young man with lanky black hair and a blade-thin face answers the door. By his bare feet, Ruth surmises he's not the broker.

"Come in and have a look," he says, and then disappears into one of the bedrooms, where a television is playing.

Ruth steps into the living room, a long narrow space the proportions of a tunnel, the light at the end of which is a single casement window. The furnishings are spare and missing cushions and legs. Japanese cartoon posters are stapled to the walls. Though Ruth has never been inside a fraternity house, she imagines this is the décor. She peers into the kitchen. It isn't wide enough to turn around in. She inspects the bathroom—no tub, only a shower. A large tea-color rust stain encircles the drain. She wanders into the first bedroom, empty save for an unmade bed. The barefoot young man didn't bother to make his bed for the open house? She heads into the second bedroom, astounded to find it crowded—Alex, the barefoot young man biting his nails, two Russian gentlemen in camel-hair coats, a couple with a baby, and the young woman who, only yesterday, asked to lie down on their bed. Ruth recognizes the knee-high boots. All eyes are on the young man's television, a vast flat screen that fills one entire wall. The basset-eyed newscaster's face is as large as the moon. He wears the expression of an oracle about to make a prediction. Across his brow is written *Breaking News—Target: New York City.* "Fifteen thousand yellow cabs service New York at any given hour," he says. "Let's face it, every cab is now a potential ground zero."

"What happened?" Ruth asks.

"Pamir's carjacked a taxi," Alex tells her.

"Who can tell one rag-head cabbie from another? They'll never catch him now," says one of the Russians.

"Maybe he's heading back to the tunnel to finish the job?" says the other.

Ruth recognizes the "the sky is falling" tactic to scare away the competition. The Russians are what her father—a dreamy, deeply religious egg peddler who refused to make an extra nickel off the World War II black market—

used to call war gonifs. Her mother called her father the village schlemiel.

"Maybe he's driving out of town and will become someone else's problem?" says the nail-biting young man.

"Maybe he's going to Queens. Isn't his wife in Queens?" says the thoughtless girl in the knee-high boots.

"Don't they have the cab's medallion number?" Ruth asks.

"Pamir locked the driver in the trunk. They don't know which cab it is," Alex says.

"The mayor's ordered all taxis back to their garages by ten," says knee-high boots.

"Pamir still has forty-eight minutes to go," says the first Russian. "And who knows if he's acting alone? A lot could still happen."

"He can make himself a few dollars on fares and tips before he blows himself up," says the other.

"Or *gives* himself up," says the nail-biting young man.

Lily was right, Ruth thinks, the television news shouldn't be on during an open house.

A satellite image of Manhattan shimmers on the screen. The grid of streets is golden-yellow, the buildings infrared squares. The basset-eyed newscaster turns to his newest guest, "Professor and Author of *The Universal Theory of Traffic*." "How do you get fifteen thousand cabs off the streets by ten o'clock?"

The professor's beard is so thick and wild he appears to be peeking over a hedge. "You don't," he says, turning around to face the satellite image: the back of his head looks exactly like the front, but without eyes. "Traffic behaves like liquid. Think of the infrared squares as islands, and the yellow grid as tributaries. Imagine each taxicab is a drop of water suddenly moving against the tide. Rip currents might occur, backing up traffic for hours, gigantic waves could flood intersections."

The basset-eyed newscaster, who's been listening with the solemnity of a bright, if cloying student, faces his audience again, the tableau of house hunters crowded around the screen. "New York is beautiful from outer space, folks, but today, that golden grid isn't made up of yellow brick roads."

"Maybe it's not such a wise idea to go apartment hunting today," Alex says as they exit the pink lobby.

"Maybe it's the wisest time of all to go hunting. Did you see the poor seller's face when everyone but the Russians left? He looked ready to give away his apartment. I hope we didn't look like that yesterday."

As soon as they reach the corner, and can see in all four directions, Alex checks if the color cadmium yellow dark has disappeared from the otherwise gray cityscape, but Yellow Cabs are still plentiful. He watches a woman come out of the Lower East Side Bake Shoppe and hail one, so enjoying the muffin she is eating that she doesn't bother to check if Pamir is her driver or not. Alex wants what that woman's eating, a muffin so tasty you forget reason.

"Let's sit down somewhere warm, Ruth, enjoy a muffin and a cup of coffee, and wait until ten. It's almost a quarter to. Once the cabs are off the streets, we're bound to know more."

As they step into the bakery, the same acuity he had

with hearing earlier, he now has with smell. He can distinguish cinnamon, sugar, coffee, burned caraway seeds, toasted wheat and earthy bran.

"A bran muffin and a coffee," he says to the woman behind the counter.

"You sure you want a bran muffin *and* a coffee?" Ruth asks. "You don't want an English muffin instead?"

"The world may end today, I want a bran muffin."

"A tea and an English muffin for me, please," she says.

They eat at a table by the window. Alex yanks down his muffin's waxed-paper skirt while Ruth sugars her tea. "I hope we can still get to the hospital today," she says, adding another spoonful. "Do you think Dorothy somehow knows we're coming?"

"She knows." He takes a big bite, stunned at how good it tastes. It's as saturated with flavors as the air is with scents. He chews with concentration and pleasure, and as he does, he remembers relishing a pumpernickel loaf between skirmishes on the German border, how fear had made everything taste so good.

"Oh my," Ruth says.

He looks up from his muffin and follows her surprised gaze out the window. There isn't a Yellow Cab in sight. It's as if he's seeing a dear old friend he'd known only in a blond toupee, suddenly bald. He turns to the man at the next table, hunched over a laptop. "Can you get the news on that?"

Without so much as glancing up to see what might be going on outside, the man reads his screen. "Police just found Pamir's taxi abandoned under the FDR near the Queensboro Bridge."

"How do they know its Pamir's?" Alex asks.

"The cabbie was still in the trunk."

"Alive?"

"Yes."

"Pamir?" Ruth asks.

"Long gone."

Ruth would like nothing more than to go home and climb under the covers until it's safe to visit Dorothy, but she's also anxious to see the other apartment before anything else happens. She suspects that her anxiety isn't only because Pamir's still out there. On the contrary, had he been caught, there would be no rush to look at the built-in bookcases and window seat on their way to the hospital; they could no longer afford them. As ashamed as she is to admit it, she's a little relieved he's still out there.

She rises from her chair. "Let's go look at the other apartment."

"I haven't finished my muffin," Alex says.

"You can finish it on the way."

On the corner of Second Avenue and Second Street, Ruth realizes that the apartment shares the block with the old cemetery, a half-acre sanctuary of trees, marble headstones, stone walls, a wrought-iron gate, and a plaque that reads: *Marble Cemetery* 1830—*A Place of Internment for Gentlemen.* Living on the same street as the cemetery is even better than living near the park. These gentlemen don't ride skateboards and play boom boxes. She quickens her stride. The building is on the south side, catching all the sun. It's still a half dozen doors away, but she can already see it overlooks the sanctuary. She tamps down her excitement. They haven't even been inside. The façade is nothing to speak of—standard turn-of-the-century brick—but the exterior has been recently painted, a tasteful sand color with black trim. The front door is rosewood. The directory is framed under glass: all the names are neatly typed. She presses the intercom bell beside the realtor's card. "We're here for the open house," she shouts into the speaker.

"Take the elevator to the top floor and turn right," the intercom answers back with crystal clarity.

The lobby is simple but attractive; black and white tiles, wainscoting, white walls, and a small French Provincial bench. She rings for the elevator. When the door opens, a fox terrier trots out, followed by a preoccupied man talking on a cell phone.

"Dogs must be allowed!" Ruth says to Alex.

The elevator is slow, but steady. The sixth-floor walls are the same cream white as the lobby. The corridor is so quiet Ruth can hear blood banging in her ears. She knocks on the apartment door. The realtor, a tall young woman in a black bubble haircut, invites them inside. Ruth's sure she smells something delicious baking until she realizes it's only boiled cinnamon. Alex wanders into the bedrooms to see if one would make a good studio, while she starts in the living room, curious to see the floor-to-ceiling bookcases and the built-in window seat. The room is already crowded with milling overcoats and gleaming, overheated faces and wet shoes, and one familiar pair of knee-high boots. No one seems alarmed by the latest news; they seem far more interested in the crown molding. But then again, the television is off. She sits down on the window seat's Chinese red cushion. The view is just what she hoped it would be: sanctuary and sky.

The kitchen is tinier than she'd like, but there's a square of morning sun on the floor for Dorothy to sunbathe in. She tests the stove: all four burners work.

The first bedroom is about the same size as the one they have now, more than enough room for a queen-size bed, two night tables, and a computer desk. From the window, she can see the branches of a majestic oak, bare and black. In summer, the whole view will be verdant. She's tempted to lie down on the bed to see the view from there, but, of course, she doesn't dare. Besides, the girl, sans her knee-high boots, is already lying there.

The second bedroom catches Ruth off-guard; it's such an irregular shape, a trapezoid with one long wall and three short ones. She's no judge of distance, but the farthest wall appears to be over twenty feet away, or perhaps it's just a spatial illusion. Alex is staring across the length of the room to that white wall just waiting for a blank canvas. He takes a giant stride backward, and then another and another. The studio he has now is only fifteen feet long. She knows what those extra five feet would mean for him.

A line has already formed to talk to the realtor. While they wait their turn, Alex feels the same roiling want for the vista of wall that Ruth feels for the verdant view, but in his case, he suspects that the churning might also be from the bran muffin with the coffee chaser. "I may have to use the bathroom," he whispers to Ruth.

"Now? We're next in line. You can't wait?"

"I'm sorry."

"How can I help you?" says the realtor.

"How firm is the price?" Ruth asks.

"I'll be right back," Alex promises, and hurries down the hall looking for a bathroom. Despite the million-one price tag, the apartment only seems to have one, and two young Asian women taking pictures of the tub with their cell phones occupy it.

"Please, I need to use the bathroom," Alex says. He locks himself inside and opens the window as wide as it will go. The cold is shocking. He releases his belt and sits down on the commode.

Someone knocks.

"I'll be right out!" he shouts.

Someone taps.

"Just a minute!"

Someone hammers.

"Hold your horses!"

To ignore the knocks, he turns off his hearing aids and concentrates on the floor. The tile work is handsome, a diamond pattern. Four black squares framed in eight blue-green ones. How would he mix the color? Cerulean with viridian? With a vista like that, he could paint larger. If the FBI memos evoked illuminated manuscripts, why not billboards?

When he finishes, he flushes the toilet, closes the seat, washes his hands, tucks in his shirt, turns up his hearing aids, and then scours his pockets for matches, but all he finds is the packet of Stim-U-Dents. He leaves the window open, unlocks the door, and squeezes past the knot of house hunters waiting to see what a million-one bathroom is like.

Ruth ran out of questions for the realtor long ago. She sits on the window seat cushion, her back to the view, waiting for Alex. When he finally shows up, she says, "It's a sealed auction. Bids are being accepted till noon. The results will be final. We sign a contract. No second chances. No backing out."

"I'm sorry, I couldn't wait," he says.

"I told you to have an English muffin. Next time will you listen?"

In the elevator, on their way down to the lobby to call Lily in private, Ruth takes his arm with conciliatory tenderness. "Hey, you never know, you might have turned the odds in our favor by overpowering the smell of cinnamon."

"We can call it the Bran Muffin Principle," Alex says.

In the lobby, Ruth dials Lily.

"No one is making anymore commitments until Pamir's caught," Lily tells her.

Ruth lowers the phone. "Yellow Rubbers' is our last solid offer, nine even."

"Ask her advice," Alex says.

"We found a place, Lily, it's perfect. We have to put our bid in before noon or we'll lose it. The sellers are asking a million one, but the realtor says the seller is willing to consider any offer. Any words of wisdom?"

"If the seller is willing to consider *any* offer, it means he's scared, which might work in your favor. Take advantage, but don't bid so low that if you lose it, you kick your-selves for not risking more, and don't bid so high that if you get it, you have to back out. That could cost you *real* money in legal fees. And make sure everyone signs the bid contract. If Pamir turns out not to be a terrorist, just a nut-case, the seller might use any excuse to wheedle out of the agreement. Lots of buyers include a personal letter with their offer, an appeal to the seller why they should be cho-sen in the event of a tie. If you write one, don't be afraid to pull on the heartstrings. We realtors call it a Queen-for-a-Day letter."

When Ruth first retired, she thought she'd try her hand at writing. Nothing as ambitious as fiction—she hardly believed she'd find an untapped vein of talent—but auto-biographical sketches or profiles of people she had known, exercises written just for herself, an experiment to see if her love of reading could translate into something more. To her frustration and then disenchantment, what she under-stood as a reader—the bracing delight of the unexpected metaphor, the fascination with spying on another's con-sciousness—eluded her as soon as she splayed her fingers across the typewriter keys. She typed clichés. She was like the old illiterate peasant woman in Chekhov's "At Christ-mas Time," dictating a letter to her daughter, who she hasn't heard from in years. She timidly asks the scribe to write down a string of platitudes—"to our only beloved daughter, our love, a low bow and our parental blessing enduring forever and ever. And we also send wishes for a merry Christmas, we are alive and well, and hoping you are the same, please God, the Heavenly King"—when what the old peasant really means to tell her daughter is that she and Grandpa had to sell the cow and are now starving.

In an odd way, Ruth felt relieved to put away her ambition—a part of her had always worried that teaching had kept her from a greater destiny, and now she knew. She never told Alex about her exercises. That winter, she ran for secretary of the local chapter of Women for Peace and Justice and accepted her lot as a pamphleteer.

But now, sitting on the bench in the lobby, it seems to her she has one last chance to put her story on paper.

Dear Sellers,
Our day began with a miracle. The doctors told us our little dog, Dorothy, might never walk again, but this morning, she took five steps. We're hoping for a second miracle today, that you chose us in the event of a tie. My husband, a renowned artist, and I, a retired public school teacher, have lived in this neighborhood for nearly forty-five years. It would mean so much to us if we didn't have to leave at our age. We adore your apartment, especially the window seat and the built-in bookcases. The second bedroom will make an ideal studio for my husband, and our little dog can regain her strength sunbathing on your kitchen tiles.
Yours,
Alex and Ruth Cohen

She rereads the letter. It's the truth, but it reads like propaganda.

"How much?" she asks Alex.

"We should make it an even trade. Write down nine hundred thousand," he says. But as soon as she agrees and plies her pen to the contract, he changes his mind. "Make it nine hundred and ten. We can manage another ten, Ruth. Rudolph said he's getting traction on my FBI pieces. No, write down nine hundred and twenty thousand; no, nine hundred and thirty . . ."

Ruth knows that the amounts he's dictating to her are like the old peasant woman's prayers, that what he really means to say is: *We've put the cow up for sale. Don't we deserve some peace?*

She finally writes *$950,000,* an amount she doesn't believe she's ever written down before. When would she have had the opportunity?

BARKS, HOWLS, YAPS, AND YELPS RESOUND UP and down the hospital's corridors. Inside her cage, Dorothy listens with apathy and distain. She has no interest in adding her voice to the bedlam. She stares through the bars and whimpers, a mournful hum lost in the din. It's finally sunk in that this is her life now, a cell in a windowless ward, noisy with other dogs' ranting, where her only treat is a teensy crumble of sausage.

"They've been going berserk for the past ten minutes," says the orderly as he hoses out the empty cage below Dorothy's; the bulldog finally passed the penny. "They know something's up. They can smell danger. We should listen to them instead of the newscasters. You didn't see any pictures of elephants drowned in the tsunami, did you?"

"I heard a parrot just got loose in pre-op and tried to fly through the glass door," says the medical student as he administers nose spray to the Mexican hairless.

"They have a sixth sense."

"They're only smelling your fear," says the nurse as she opens Dorothy's cage door. She picks her up. "You're not a scaredy-cat, are you?" She gently wipes away the jelled tears caked under Dorothy's eyes. "Your mommy and daddy are here. You don't want them to think you were crying. Look at those long beautiful lashes. Who does your makeup?"

Cradling Dorothy in her arms, the nurse carries her through a maze of hallways until they arrive at a big room pungent with outdoor smells—snow, slush, wet leather, damp wool, goose down, fur, feathers, and hair. After the overpowering odors of her ward mates, it's like a bouquet.

"I'm looking for Dorothy's owners," the nurse asks the receptionist.

"The little old couple? They're in visiting Room two."

Holding Dorothy in one hand, the nurse opens a door. Ruth and Alex rise from two plastic chairs. They look anything but little and old to Dorothy. To Dorothy, they look like titans. She recognizes Ruth's glasses first, the enormous omnipotent eyes, and then Alex's outstretched hands, those quick, strong hands that always sweep her up when bigger dogs approach.

"Ruth, she's wagging her tail!"

The tiny room becomes heady with the sharp, sweet scent of reunion. Alex carefully takes Dorothy from the nurse and then shares her with Ruth. Dorothy is cushioned between their soft overcoats, in a bough of arms. She inhales the essences of Alex and Ruth. She kisses their coat sleeves, buttons, fingers, wristwatches, and when Ruth leans closer, her nose and glasses.

RUTH HAS TO FORCE HERSELF TO LOOK AT the shaved clearing in the fur, the silver railroad tracks running along the crest of Dorothy's spine—a five-inch incision fastened with staples. The staples look painful to Ruth, but Dorothy doesn't seem to notice them. Settling into Ruth's arms, she lets loose a sigh of such contentment that Ruth feels it though her sleeves, through her skin.

"She's so light, Alex. I think she lost weight."

"We'd like to talk to Dr. Rush," he tells the nurse as she leaves.

They sit down to wait for the doctor, Dorothy on Ruth's lap. The whole time in the bus, she and Alex had to stand. At every stop, surges of passengers would push and ebb like tides. The taxis were still under curfew, though Ruth has no idea why. Isn't Pamir on foot again?

Alex puts one arm around her, the other around Dorothy. Stirring on her lap, Dorothy looks up at her, and then turns her doleful, intelligent eyes on Alex. Though Dorothy can't give voice to the look, Ruth knows what it means: *Don't ever leave me again.*

The doctor comes in. "You wanted to see me?"

"Are the staples painful?" Ruth asks.

"Animals feel pain differently than we do."

"When we get her home, is there anything else we can do besides crate her?" Alex asks.

"I advise five hundred milligrams of glucosamine daily, also chrondroitin. Some owners swear by vitamin C and beta-carotene. There's also a promising new drug called Adequan."

"We'll have to clear off another shelf in the medicine cabinet for her," Alex says.

"Can she still run around if she's able?" Ruth asks.

"Just let her be a dog." He waits for another question, but Ruth and Alex can't think of one. "The nurse will be coming for Dorothy in a few minutes. I'd let her go home with you now, but after that seizure I'd like to keep her one more night."

When he closes the door behind him, Ruth says, "I almost forgot about the seizure."

Alex pats her shoulder, caresses Dorothy's neck, and then looks at his wristwatch. "The auction's been over for nearly ten minutes."

"I turned off the cell phone. We're not supposed to use it in the hospital."

"Should I see if there's a pay phone?"

"We almost lost her, Alex. What difference will knowing five minutes later make? We either got the apartment or we didn't." She turns her attention to Dorothy. "We brought you something, sweetie." She reaches into her purse and takes out the rubber hot dog, but Dorothy ignores it. "Those staples must hurt her. How does the doctor know that her pain feels different than ours?"

Alex continues rubbing Ruth's shoulder and stroking Dorothy's neck. Gliding back and forth against the dark fur, his shiny wristwatch hypnotizes Ruth: it's almost twelve-thirty. "Where's the nurse already?" she asks.

Barks explode from all the wards along the green corridor as the nurse carries Dorothy, listless and silent, back to her cell. Dorothy's sixth sense—a tactile alarm, as if danger were a breeze moving through her fur—is as strong as the next dog's; she's aware of the mounting agitation in the air, but she's too forlorn to care; Ruth and Alex just handed her away.

"They're getting louder by the minute," the orderly says to the nurse as he changes the yelping, shrieking Mexican hairless's water bowl. "I'm telling you, they know something."

The nurse opens Dorothy's cage and settles her inside, like a loaf of soft dough laid in an oven. Dorothy's instinct is to stand up and bark, too, to become one with the pack, to howl her head off until every dog in the land is alerted to the danger, but her sadness prevails: she curls into a ball and holds her tongue.

"You and me are the only one keeping our heads, aren't we, Dorothy?" says the nurse, locking her inside.

In the hospital lobby, beside a wall of donor plaques honoring departed pets—in memory of Stretch, Buttons, Chaos, Irving—Ruth and Alex check their cell phone to see if the realtor has left a message, though if she has, neither knows how retrieve it. The bright plasma bar reads fifty-eight new messages, one more than this morning. Ruth dials the realtor, while Alex glances out the lobby doors to see if the taxis are back. Flashing red glyphs and whirling blue lances play over the glass. Two helmeted silhouettes flank the entry. The doors spring open and a frantic woman clutching a shoe box rushes in.

"Has something happened?" Alex asks her.

"My ferret just went crazy and jumped out the second story window. I think he's broken his leg."

"The FBI's got Pamir trapped in Bed Bath and Beyond just around the corner," says the moon-faced young guard manning the metal detector. He steps in front of the woman and holds up his hand like a crossing guard. "You'll have to open the box," he says.

"You think I have a bomb in here?"

"Otherwise, the box has to go through X-ray."

She cracks the lid wide enough for the guard, and Alex, to see tiny white teeth. The guard lets her pass.

"Do they know if he has a bomb?" Alex asks him.

"Nope, but they know he took hostages."

"How many?"

"As many as he could grab in kitchenware."

Ruth throws her arms around Alex. "It's ours! We got the apartment! There was a tie, but our letter made the difference!" She looks out the glass doors, at the fleet of idling squad cars frenetic with red and blue lights. The two helmeted silhouettes have doubled into four. "Has something happened?"

"The FBI has Pamir cornered nearby in a Bed Bath and Beyond," Alex tells her.

"They have one on the Upper East Side?"

"It's just around the corner," the moon-faced guard pipes in.

"Does he have a bomb?" Ruth asks.

"He has hostages," Alex says.

"I don't want to leave Dorothy here with a bomb nearby. Is the hospital in any danger?" she asks the guard.

"Nobody's told me anything," the guard says.

"Pamir might not even have a bomb, Ruth. If the hospital was in any danger, the police would have evacuated it by now."

"They might evacuate the people, but will they take the animals?"

She strides past Alex and the guard, opens the door, and approaches one of the helmeted silhouettes, faceless behind a dark visor, clad in black armor, holding an assault rifle. She barely comes up to his bulletproof vest. Alex, who follows her outside, barely comes up to his chinstrap. "We're supposed to bring our little dog home tomorrow," Ruth tells the policeman, "but we can go back for her right now if you think she's in any danger. Is the hospital safe?"

"The hospital is in the green zone, ma'am."

"What's a green zone?" Ruth asks.

Alex doesn't know anymore than Ruth does, but he figures a green zone must be safer than a red zone. "She's better off in the hospital than out here," he tells Ruth as panicked pedestrians push by. "How would we get her home? There still aren't any taxis."

"Please, folks, we need to keep the walkway clear," says the faceless helmet.

To their west, beyond the fleet of squad cars, a convoy

of armored trucks, FBI vans, fire engines, a Caterpillar bulldozer with its plow raised, and ambulances block First Avenue, ready to descend on Bed Bath & Beyond. To their east, circling above the Fifty-ninth Street Bridge, helicopters drone. Civilian traffic, both heeled and wheeled, is being diverted onto York Avenue. Alex and Ruth join the downtown foot traffic being channeled between police sawhorses erected along the sidewalks. The crowd is too unwieldy to move with any flow through such a tight space. Overcoats press against them, pushing to get as far away as fast as possible. Whenever a siren goes off or horns honk the panic intensifies and Alex can feel himself and Ruth momentarily lifted off their feet and borne along by the pressure. He struggles to free his arm and wraps it protectively around her. She holds on to his waist, gripping his overcoat.

"You were so right, Alex. Thank God we left Dorothy at the hospital."

In the shadow of the Fifty-ninth Street Bridge, the police barricades abruptly end and the pressure is released. What had been a chute of crazed cattle now becomes an orderly herd. A man stops to straighten out his crushed dry cleaning. A woman answers her cell phone. Alex and Ruth, still holding on to each other, duck into a doorway to get their bearings and catch their breath. South of the bridge, the city looks relatively normal—stores are open, traffic is moving, albeit slowly. Overhead, the cable car from Roosevelt Island is still running, albeit with no one inside. Locking hands, they make their way south. Near the bridge, at the stone feet of its massive pillars, news vans are parked every which way, cables erupting from their interiors, antenna poles telescoping out of their roofs. Atop each pole, a satellite dish tilts heavenward. Cameramen and heavily powdered reporters surround a middle-aged woman in a torn pink parka clutching a Bed Bath & Beyond bag as if whatever it contained was priceless.

"I was at the checkout when everyone started screaming and running," she shouts into a thicket of microphones. Her voice is so shrill even Alex can hear her. "I got pushed on the floor and lost my glasses. Someone stepped on my coat and tore it. I forgot to get my card back and now I can't find . . ."

Before she can finish her story of loss, the cameramen pan away and focus on the bridge's exit ramp. Alex follows their aim. The lower lanes are solid yellow. Against the bridge's black shadows and the gray afternoon sky, the taxis look dazzling.

"Breaking news," announces one reporter after another, repositioning themselves before the cameras so that the bridge, with its golden vein, is now their backdrop. "The mayor has ordered all cabbies back to work. He urges New Yorkers to go about their business as usual, just avoid the Upper East Side."

"Just what we need, more traffic," grumbles someone in the crowd.

"Who would come into the city?" asks another.

"Maybe it's over," ventures a third.

The crowd suddenly fractures and people start running to catch the taxis as they pour off the bridge near Second Avenue.

Still holding hands, Ruth and Alex hurry to catch one, too.

.   .   .

"Where to?" asks the thick-necked Ukrainian cabbie glancing in his rearview mirror at Alex and Ruth. Alex takes off his baseball cap; his white hair sticks up in disarray, like an albino tornado. Ruth yanks loose her wool scarf as if it's strangling her.

"Second Avenue and Third Street, please," she tells the driver, then turns to Alex. "I told the realtor we were coming right over with our deposit."

"We shouldn't give her any money until Pamir's either caught or dead, until it's over," Alex says. "I'm not writing a check while the city's under siege." He leans forward. "St. Mark's and Avenue A," he tells the cabbie.

"We could lose the apartment," Ruth says. "You didn't talk to the realtor, I did." She leans forward, too. "Second and Third."

The cabbie turns around. His neck is so stiff and solid, it looks, to Ruth, as if only his head swivels, like a cap on a bottle.

"Just drive downtown," Alex tells him. "We'll give you the address when we get closer."

"Look at this traffic," the cabbie mutters, banging on the steering wheel. He guns the engine and lurches an inch closer to the stalled bumper in front of him. "How can the mayor order me back to work? Does he think he's my commandant? Who gave him such power?"

"Do you know what's happening with Pamir?" Alex asks. "Can you turn on the radio?"

"It's broken. Last I heard he was in that Beyond place with hostages. Look at this gridlock. That TV professor of traffic was right. He warned the mayor there'd be tidal waves and floods if he ordered the cabs back."

"We should at least call the realtor, Alex, and tell her we're still coming over with our deposit, we'll just be a little late," Ruth says.

"What is she going to do if you don't call her?"

"Phone our competition and ask if they want to make a counteroffer."

"If the tie had come out differently, and our letter lost, would you make a counteroffer right now?"

"What is it with this bus?" the cabbie mutters, gunning his engine and honking to no avail. The broad side of a double-decker Grey Line Tour bus now takes up the cab's entire windshield. Ruth can count only two sightseers inside, a man and a woman. The woman is squinting uptown toward Bed Bath & Beyond, her faced pressed to the glass, her hands cupping her eyes as if she were holding binoculars. The man is asleep beside her, head back, jaw slack.

Forty-five minutes later, despite the Ukrainian crazily changing lanes, revving in place, kissing bumpers, and relentlessly honking, the cab is only at Fourteenth Street, stuck in another swamped intersection.

"It will be faster to walk home from here," Alex says, paying the driver. "Can I get a receipt?"

On the corner, in the first lit storefront they pass, a laundromat, six souls are gathered around a small television playing on the fluff 'n' fold counter. A massive black garment fills the screen.

Alex opens the door. "Is that his mother?" he asks any-one who will answer.

"Yes, she's standing outside BB and B, talking on the phone with her son," someone says.

Ruth steps closer to the tiny screen to see with her bad eyes. The black garment is shaking and blurry. The angle must be from one of the news helicopters circling over the Upper East Side, shot with a telephoto lens: the fuzzy black shape keeps changing form.

"How long has she been talking to her son?" Ruth asks.

"They've shown the same clip for the last half hour. We don't even know if Pamir's on the line. They can't broad-cast the call because it might taint a jury later on," says a girl with a tongue stud folding her laundry while she watches.

The garment fades and the basset-eyed newscaster takes over the screen. "Only fifty-two percent of our view-ers say they'd come out if their mother called. What do the experts think?"

He's turns to the double-chinned forensic psychologist from this morning. Six hours under the hot lights and her lipstick looks as if it's melting. "The suicide bomber believes he's doing this *for* his mother," she says.

They step outside again, keep walking south. At the corner of St. Mark's, they dart into the magazine shop to see if the stout old counterman, who always sports a bow tie, has his radio on.

"Anything new?" Alex asks him.

"He still won't talk to his mother," says the counter-man.

They turn east toward home. Mr. Rahim, in only shirt-sleeves, is smoking in his open doorway. He smiles when he see them, delicately tamps out his cigarette, and inserts it back into the pack to smoke later.

"What's the latest?" Alex asks.

"According to the forensic professor lady? Or my wife?" Mr. Rahim says. "The forensic lady believes Pamir won't speak to his mother because he already has a foot in the next world and he's frightened his mother's voice might call him back. My wife thinks Pamir is too ashamed to speak to his mother. She has relatives by marriage from those same Afghanistan mountains; she says the villagers are as simple as beasts. My wife's convinced Pamir's on drugs: she thinks that stupid girl yesterday wasn't his hostage; she was his dealer."

"What do you think?" Alex asks.

"I think before Pamir took refuge in Bed Bath and Beyond, he had no bomb or weapons or leverage, and now he has steak knives and hostages. How's Miss Dottie?"

"She's coming home tomorrow," Ruth says.

"You still miss your mommy and daddy?" asks the nurse, returning with a bowl of food, Dorothy's first real meal in days. As preoccupied as her ward mates are with contributing to the barking, they also smell her food. The Mexican hairless's high notes, already shrill, go up an octave. The pug's bulbous black eyes practically pop out with each yelp.

Though Dorothy is still too despondent to have an appetite, she doesn't want these two to get her meal. She crouches over her bowl, curls back her black lips, and bears her yellow teeth. Her threat does no good. She can sense the other dogs' agitation fueling their appetites; anxiousness is making them ravenous.

Lest she have to share, Dorothy forces herself to eat. She takes a small bite and chews, and as she chews, something unexpected happens. She no longer smells the other dogs, only meat; she no longer hears the barking hysteria, only herself chewing. The circumference of her bowl might as well be the whole globe; she sees nothing else. And she no longer aches for Ruth and Alex. While she's eating, nothing else is real.

·

"I'M NOT SURPRISED PAMIR IS HOLDING HIS hostages in kitchenware," says the forensic psychologist as Alex and Ruth, shedding their overcoats, turn on their television. "Most suicide bombers target places where crowds gather for food—open markets, cafes, restaurants. Food is culture and it's our culture they want to blow up."

"Try another channel," Ruth says.

Alex switches to the next network, Fox News, a station Ruth normally refuses to watch. This afternoon, she doesn't say a word.

"One tactical possibility is the lone sniper," speculates a retired general with appallingly dyed hair. "If a sniper can crawl undetected through the air-conditioning ducts between the floors, he might get a clean shot at Pamir, without endangering the hostages."

"I hope Pamir isn't watching this in the store," Alex says.

"I don't think they sell TVs."

Alex presses ahead to the next news channel.

"Tokyo's market opens in less than the four minutes," says a beautiful Singaporean with a swan-length neck.

"How will world markets react to New York's crisis?" she asks her guest, a stock analyst with a walleye who is obviously smitten by her.

"I'm going to check the messages to see if the realtor called," Ruth says. "She must be wondering where we are?"

"If she called, it's only to pressure us," Alex calls after her as she disappears into the bedroom. "She doesn't expect anyone to bring over a check right now." He gets up and goes into the kitchen. All he's had to eat today was a bran muffin. He opens the fridge—an iceberg lettuce, tomatoes, and a grapefruit. He needs something more comforting. He opens the freezer—mushroom barley soup! From Fairway! He takes out the ice-hard container, opens the microwave, sets it on the lazy Susan, and presses high. The microwave hums loudly. He peers into its window and watches the soup twirl in place, like a ballerina in a music box.

"Where are you? I left a message on your cell. Please call me as soon as you get this," says the realtor's dry, vexed voice on their answering machine.

A second message plays, "The sellers are getting anxious. They want me to open the bidding again if you don't get here in the next ten minutes."

Not quite sure what she's going to tell the realtor—the truth, they're home, or a white lie, they're running late—Ruth reaches for the phone when it suddenly rings: she pulls back her hand as if the phone had tried to bite her.

"The other party, the ones whose letter didn't win the

tie," says the answering machine, "just phoned to say they're seriously considering making a counteroffer. Call me ASAP."

Had the realtor simply said the other party was still interested, Ruth would have believed her, but Alex is right, no one makes a counteroffer right now.

She waits a moment, and then dials the realtor back. "We're still at the animal hospital. No one's being allowed to leave. The police say it's too dangerous. Pamir is just around the corner at Bed Bath and Beyond. We're in the red zone," she says, when what she really means to tell the realtor is, *We haven't sold the cow yet. We will not be pressured.*

Ruth walks into the kitchen just as the soup ends its dance.

"Who called?" Alex asks.

"You were so right. The realtor only wants to pressure us."

She takes two bowls out of the cupboard, and then looks for the ladle. In the living room, the television begins playing the fully orchestrated *Breaking News* theme song. It might as well be a bugle calling Alex to arms. He hurries back to his post on the sofa. Despite the martial music, the screen is as motionless as a still photograph: a long shot, probably taken from a rooftop, of an eerily empty First Avenue, save for Pamir's mother, tiny against the cityscape, now surrounded by helmeted silhouettes acting as bodyguards. The black garment and her protectors progress at a very slow crawl up the avenue. She looks, to Alex, like a black insect with eighteen legs.

"You think Pamir's finally going to talk to his mother?" Ruth asks, a soup bowl in each hand. She sits beside him.

"I think his mother wants to talk to her son in person. Those policeman appear to be leading her to him," Alex says, taking his hot bowl and stirring his soup. He thinks he sees movement behind the store windows, though Pamir's mother is still a good five hundred yards away from the entrance. In the army, his job had been to spot targets for snipers.

"Do you think his mother's going to ask him to surrender?" Ruth asks.

"Why else would she go to him?"

The eighteen legs suddenly stop. The bodyguards raise their shields to envelop the black garment, like a steel carapace. A ribbon of words scrolls across the screen's bottom: *The shield material is able to withstand a projectile traveling at velocities of up to 1.5 km/second. This is approximately equivalent to dropping four diesel locomotives onto an area the size of one's fingernail.*

"What are they waiting for?" Ruth says.

"They're probably hoping to lure him out," Alex says, taking his first taste of soup. Even before the spoon reaches his lips, he suspects it's still too hot to eat, but he takes a sip anyway. He scalds his tongue, but he doesn't lose his focus. Something is happening behind the glass. The shadows are congealing into a solid entity: Pamir must be rounding up his hostages.

The phone rings. Without taking his eyes off the store window, no bigger than a postage stamp on the screen, he reaches for the phone with his free hand, but Ruth stops him.

"What if it's the realtor?" she says.

"I'll tell her what you told her: she should stop pestering us. We'll bring over the deposit as soon as It's safe go outside again," he says.

"I told her we were still at the animal hospital, in some kind of lockdown."

"Why did you lie?"

The answering machine picks up. Ruth disappears into the bedroom to listen, while Alex remains on the sofa, watching the congealed shadow. It appears to be inching toward the store's main entrance on a great many legs, too.

"We're at the beach house," says the answering machine. "Rudolph insisted we get out of the city."

Ruth lifts the receiver. "May."

"How's Dorothy?"

"She's walking. She's coming home tomorrow."

"You and Alex must be so relieved."

"You can't imagine."

"Is anything happening? Our TV isn't working. There's six feet of snow on the roof. Rudolph's on the ladder right now trying to fix the cable. I told him he'd have been safer staying the city and shopping at Bed Bath and Beyond."

"I think Pamir's about to give himself up. His mother is standing outside the store right now," Ruth says.

"Rudolph!" May shouts. "Get off the ladder and pick up the other extension. I'm on the phone with Ruth. Pamir is about to turn himself in."

Ruth takes the cordless back into the living room.

"Is it the realtor?" Alex asks.

"May. Their TV isn't working."

Ruth sits beside him on the sofa and straightens her

glasses. "Nothing's happening," she tells May. "His mother and her bodyguards are still standing in the middle of the street."

"Look at the window," Alex says, pointing to the screen.

It's a long shot of an empty First Avenue. There must be a thousand windows. "Which window?"

"The one directly below the Beyond sign."

Ruth now sees the shadow, too. "Something's going on in the store," she tells May.

The shadow slowly disappears from the window and reappears just behind the entry doors.

"I think he's coming out with the hostages," Ruth tells May.

"Or maybe he's trading the hostages for his mother," Alex says, picking up the living room extension.

"What kind of trade is that?" Rudolph asks, picking up his end.

Suddenly, glass appears to blow apart exactly where the shadow had stood. Ruth's sure a bomb went off. "Oh my God," she mutters before realizing that the flash of glass was only the automatic doors springing open.

"He blew himself up?" Rudolph asks.

"God help us," May says.

"No, no," Ruth says. "Nothing's happened."

The shadow begins stepping into the daylight. Ruth can now distinguish separate beings, ten terrified human shields.

"The hostages are coming out," she tells May and Rudolph, "but we don't know if Pamir is hiding behind them or back in the store."

"What does the newscaster think?" May asks.

"He's quiet for once," Ruth says.

"He doesn't know anymore than we do," Alex offers.

"When has that stopped him before?" Rudolph asks.

Alex points to the screen as if all four of them can see it. "Pamir's directly behind the two women in front. See how stiffly they're walking, as if they're on a single leash."

"Where's his mother?" May asks.

"Why don't they just shoot him," Rudolph says.

The hostages come to a jerky standstill just outside the store. Their backs are to Pamir; their terrified visages face Ruth and Alex. No one moves, not even to shift their weight. One woman appears to be praying. Slowly, from behind the frieze of petrified grimaces, a hand emerges waving a white bath towel.

"He's surrendering!" Ruth gasps, expecting helmeted silhouettes to dash over and free the hostages, but no one approaches. "Why doesn't someone do something?"

"They're not doing anything?" Rudolph asks.

"He may have a bomb," Alex answers.

"Please dear God," May whispers.

A second hand rises above the hostages' heads.

"Pamir has both hands up," comments the newscaster, as if Ruth couldn't see the second hand for herself.

"What did he say?" Rudolph asks.

"Pamir's hands are up; he's getting ready to surrender," Alex says.

"Does that mean he can't press the button?" May asks.

"What button?" Rudolph says.

The shell of hostages suddenly cracks around Pamir, and the dazed men and women half run, half stumble toward helmeted silhouettes ready to shield them.

"The hostages are free," Alex tells Rudolph and May.

Pamir's alone on the sidewalk. Keeping his hands above his head, he drops to his knees and lets go of the towel. Ruth can't take her eyes off the towel, so clean and white on the filthy gray sidewalk beside the kneeling figure. Pamir looks around for, Ruth assumes, his mother. In the lower corner of the screen, she notices a dog, a Belgian shepherd, sitting patiently beside its handler, a short woman in army fatigues. The soldier unclips the dog's lead and the shepherd bounds toward Pamir, past the fleeing hostages with their shielded escorts. With fearless curiosity and relentless thoroughness, the dog circles Pamir, sniffing under his coat, in his pockets, up his sleeves, around his crotch. Pamir wears the same petrified grimace as his hostages.

"This Israeli-trained K-nine bomb sniffer is able to detect over twenty different kinds of explosives," comments the newscaster.

"What's he saying about Israel?" Rudolph asks.

When the dog is finished, it lies still as a sphinx on the pavement beside Pamir.

"Does he have a bomb?" May asks.

"We don't know. The dog is just lying there," Ruth says.

"What dog?" Rudolph asks.

"If Pamir had a bomb, the handler would have called the dog back," Alex says.

"These K-nine bomb sniffers have a ninety-six percent success rate," comments the newscaster.

"What about the other four percent?" Ruth asks.

The screen's bottom is now darkening with armored equipment, as if the picture were going black from the bottom up. Ruth can't distinguish machinery from men. Pamir remains on his knees, but he's alone now.

Where's the dog? she thinks.

A bullhorn blasts, but before Ruth can make out what's being said the words break into echoes against the buildings. Pamir lowers his hands and begins struggling to open his coat, a puffy, hooded gray parka that almost reaches his knees. He tugs at the zipper, but he can't seem to undo it. The teeth appear to be caught on something. In his panic to get the coat open, he pulls on the zipper as if it is a ripcord and he is in freefall. Ruth can't tell if the camera is running in slow motion, or her mind is, but Pamir seems to be fighting with his zipper for an eternity.

Suddenly, white feathers appear to hang in the air all around him. Only when the feathers settle does Ruth realize Pamir's ripped his parka in two to get it off. He pulls what remains of it over his head. Ruth can see he isn't strapped with explosives. The bullhorn barks again, and Pamir tosses his coat into the street. He peels off his sweater, unbuttons his shirt, and throws them on top. Clad only in a T-shirt, he slowly rises to his feet and removes his sneakers and socks, flings them into the pile, too. "The pants," the bullhorn barks. He undoes his belt, zipper, and steps out of his pants. Shivering, he kicks them away with his bare foot. He pulls his T-shirt over his head, and leaves his hands up in the air, but the bullhorn's not satisfied. It barks and barks until he takes off his underwear and lies down on the ground, spread-eagle. The station discreetly covers his derriere with what looks like a smear of Vaseline.

DOROTHY HEARS HUMAN WHOOPS, A BRONX whistle, and a burst of applause resound from the hospital corridor.

"You notice how quiet the dogs are?" says the orderly to the nurse as she stops by to check on her charges. "They stopped barking a minute ago. They knew he was going to surrender before anyone else did."

"I wonder if Bed Bath and Beyond is going to have a sale now," the nurse says, peering in on the suddenly hiccupping Mexican hairless. Despite the racket of human jubilance, Dorothy can hear shrill asthmatic bursts coming from the back of its cage, a sound her rubber hot dog makes when she bites down on it.

The nurse reaches in to comfort the creature. "If the hiccupping doesn't go away in the next half hour, call Dr. Rush."

She stops in front the pug's cage. Eyes half closed, sitting up like a meditating buddha, its clownish expression looks almost transcendent. "I think he passed out from all the exertion."

She looks in on Dorothy. Dorothy's tail starts wildly

thumping. She's hoping Ruth and Alex have come back for her now that the danger has passed.

"Look how happy she is," the orderly says. "You can smell it's over, can't you, Dorothy?"

"I TOLD YOU PAMIR NEVER HAD A BOMB TO begin with," Rudolph says.

"Thank God no one was hurt," May says.

"Who is this guy?" Alex asks.

"He's a *meshuggenah,*" Rudolph says.

"Better a lunatic than a terrorist," Alex says.

"Who says so?" Rudolph asks. "Am I to celebrate because a lunatic, not a terrorist, rammed a tanker truck into the Midtown Tunnel?"

"Yes!" May says emphatically.

Ruth understands what May doesn't; that the men's banter is the Jewish equivalent of *thank God no one was hurt.* She wants to join the camaraderie, to celebrate with the people she loves that they all survived to live another day, but Lily's pronouncement keeps haunting her, *If Pamir turns out not to be a terrorist, just a nutcase, the seller might use any excuse to wheedle out of the agreement.*

"We have to go," she interrupts the others.

"Are you sure it's safe to go out yet?" May asks.

"We found an apartment. Our offer's been accepted, but we didn't want to give them any money while Pamir was on the loose."

"You still want to buy in the city after today?" May asks. "Maybe you shouldn't rush into anything."

"It was a false alarm, why shouldn't they buy?" Rudolph says.

"Because the false alarms are as bad for our health as the real ones."

"How much was the offer?" Rudolph asks.

"Nine hundred and fifty thousand," Alex says.

"How much was the asking price?"

"One million one."

"You better hurry before the seller changes his mind," Rudolph says.

While Alex puts on his coat, Ruth dials the realtor to tell her they're on their way. "Turn off the television," she calls to Alex in the living room, "we're supposed to be at the hospital."

Ruth marches double-time down St. Mark's Place, while Alex pauses on their stoop to look around. He's not exactly sure what he expects—neighbors hugging, strangers smiling, people opening their apartment windows and shouting, as they do after winning a world series or a world war—but Avenue A is astonishingly subdued, even for a Sunday afternoon. People must be celebrating in front of their televisions.

He hurries to catch up with Ruth as she strides past Sahara's. Mr. Rahim is alone, sitting at a table like a customer, legs crossed at the knees, old-world gentleman style. He's relighting the cigarette he put in his pocket earlier. He must have been saving it for just this occasion. Alex waves at him as they rush by.

On the corner of First, he sees the platinum blond Korean manicurist in the open doorway of Lulu's Nails talking on her cell phone. He smiles at her and she smiles back. On St. Mark's, a Chinese deliveryman almost pedals into them while dialing a number. As they hurry down Second, Alex notices that every single driver appears to be talking to himself.

"Everyone in New York is on a cell phone," he says to Ruth.

"Maybe they don't want to celebrate alone."

The realtor's card is no longer taped next to the bell, but Ruth hardly needs a card to remember which apartment number it is. She presses the intercom buzzer, waits, listens, and presses again. "Hello? Anyone there? My husband and I are here with the deposit!"

Nothing.

"Are you sure you have the right apartment?" Alex asks.

"I'm positive," she says, ringing again. "Hello! Anyone there! Your realtor told us to meet her here."

Deep inside the intercom's throat, Ruth thinks she hears faint breathing. The speaker is quiet, but it's not dead. "Do you hear that?" she whispers to Alex, but he looks puzzled. She listens again to the muffled exhalations coming through the wires. "Someone's there, Alex."

Alex takes charge of the buzzer. He presses twice, holding down the button an extra measure on the last ring. "Hello! Hello! We're here to buy the apartment."

"I know who you are," the intercom finally answers. It's

a woman's voice, icy and clear. "The realtor isn't here yet. You can wait outside for her."

The speaker goes dead.

"Why isn't she letting us in? Do you think they have another buyer? I'm calling the realtor," Ruth says, opening her purse.

"Wait. Someone's coming out of the elevator," Alex says.

Ruth peers into the vestibule glass. The spiky black and white fox terrier trots across the lobby toward her. Two steps behind, in slow motion by comparison, ambles the owner on his cell phone. He's so absorbed in his conversation that he doesn't notice Ruth and Alex walk right past him as he opens the front door. "Thank you!" she calls after him once they are safely inside; the co-op members still need to approve them.

They ride the elevator up to the sixth floor. In the silent hallway, Alex's knocking on the apartment door sounds like hammering. A wink of light appears in the peephole, but the doorknob doesn't turn. Alex raps one last time as a sharp reminder that they're not giving up.

"Let me try," Ruth whispers to him, and then faces the peephole and smiles, as if her picture is about to be taken. "Hello," she says in her warmest speaking voice, as if a door isn't between them. "One of your neighbors, a gentleman with a fox terrier, kindly let us into the building. I hope you don't mind. May we come in? Please."

The door slowly cracks open and a very tall, very pregnant woman, middle-aged and furious, blocks the entry. "Your timing is awfully convenient," she says.

Ruth doesn't recognize her: she must not have attended her own open house.

"They're *finally* here," the wife shouts to her husband in the living room.

Alex spreads his fingers, like a starfish, against the open door lest the wife try to close it on them.

"Please, may we wait inside?" Ruth asks. The backlit pregnant shape doesn't move. "We would have been here sooner, but the police wouldn't let us leave the animal hospital. It's just around the corner from Bed Bath and Beyond. We were visiting our little dog, didn't the realtor tell you?"

"Don't pretend you were at the hospital. We called the hospital. I bet you don't even have a dog, let alone a crippled one."

"Of course we have a dog," Ruth says. "She's a little dachshund named Dorothy who just had back surgery."

"I spoke to the hospital receptionist," shouts the husband from the sofa. "She never heard of any lockdown."

"It's a big hospital," Ruth says. "We were on the surgical floor. Maybe the receptionist was in another wing."

The elevator opens and the realtor steps out, briefcase in hand. "Sorry. Traffic's worse now than when Pamir was on the loose. I hope no one was waiting long."

"We have the check," Alex says.

"Good. Let's get down to business." She strides past the wife into the apartment. Ruth and Alex follow. Ruth knows she shouldn't smile when she sees the window seat, but she can't help herself. The husband, a dainty-boned fifty-year-old in a red cardigan, refuses to shake her or Alex's hand when the realtor introduces them. Alex opens his wallet and takes out the check.

"What if we refuse to accept their deposit?" the husband asks the realtor.

"They've been holding us hostage all afternoon," the wife says. "Sure, now that everything's over, they're here."

"What if we want to open the bidding again?"

"We can prove they weren't at the hospital."

The realtor interrupts. "You all signed a contract to abide by the auction rules. It'll be up to the courts at this point. It could drag on for months, years. In the end, everyone loses but the lawyers. Is that what you want?" she asks her clients. She opens her briefcase and takes out a form, Acknowledgment of Earnest Money Deposit, and a pen advertising the name of her company, City Cribs.

Ruth doesn't even read the form. She signs it with the same penmanship she used to sign her students' report cards and hands the pen to Alex. He writes his name with a flourish, as if he's signing one of his paintings, and then hands the pen to the husband. He reads every word on the form, shaking his head as if they are all lies. He signs his name as if he is signing a false confession, and then holds out the pen to his wife. She looks at him as if he's betrayed her, grabs the pen, and signs it as if she is signing his death warrant.

"When are you expecting?" Ruth asks, trying to break the insufferable tension in the air. "Is it a boy or a girl?"

"Twins."

As they wait for the elevator, Ruth still feels the other couple's rage permeating the air, like a musky odor clinging to her clothes. "Can you believe the wife accused us of making up a crippled dog?" she asks Alex.

"Why did you lie about the hospital in the first place? For God's sake, Ruth, we could have lost the apartment."

"I'm sorry."

In the elevator, she takes his cold hand. "I said I was sorry. With all that was going on, it never occurred to me that they'd call the hospital."

"I bet they never did," he says.

"You think?"

When the elevator door opens in the lobby, the fox terrier looks up at them.

Ruth reaches down to pat the dog's head. "What's his name?" she asks the owner.

"Garth."

"We're going to be neighbors. We have a little dog, too. A dachshund named Dorothy."

"I'm afraid Garth can be a beast with smaller dogs. We'll have to introduce them on neutral territory."

"I understand completely," Ruth says. "Dorothy is a bit canine phobic, too."

She knows she should stop petting Garth now and let the poor man be on his way, but stroking Garth's fur is like a balm. Until the wife signed, Ruth was certain her needless lie had cost them the apartment.

They stand beside the cemetery wall, their backs to the graves, looking up at their new home.

"How should we celebrate?" Ruth asks. "Want to get a drink somewhere? Try one of the new wine bars?"

"No," he says.

"How about the Bavarian pastry shop May told us about?"

"No."

"Where would you like to go?"

"Home. I'd like to celebrate by taking a nap."

"A nap does sound good," Ruth admits.

On the stairs, trying to keep up with Alex, she says, "You really think they never called the hospital in the first place?"

"They were glued to their TV set just like we were. They never called any hospital."

"Then why were they so angry?"

"Because we didn't pay their asking price."

As soon as they walk in, Ruth checks their answering machine. "Lily hasn't called. Should we worry?"

Though it's only four-thirty, their east-facing bedroom is already in twilight. Ruth turns on the lamp, and then takes off her shoes and socks, sweater and skirt, and brassiere. She slides under the covers. Alex stretches out beside her atop the bedspread, supine and fully dressed, save for his shoes. He immediately falls asleep, but not Ruth. It's the hour when a sixty-watt bulb can usurp the power of the dying sun and turn windows into mirrors. Why did she lie? She reaches for her *Portable Chekhov* and opens to the story that was so much on her mind today, *At Christmas Time.* Curious to see why it had haunted her, she rereads it—the old peasant's visit to the scribe, the bewildered wife dictating the letter to their daughter, and then kicking herself afterward for not mentioning that grandpa is ailing, the flour bins are empty, and the cow sold. Chekhov's irony is that it wouldn't have mattered if the old woman had told her daughter the truth because the daughter is even worse off than her parents, living in squalor with a wife-beating husband and three babies.

Ruth closes the book and douses the light. What good would the truth have accomplished?

"WHEN DID SHE DIE?" ASKS THE NURSE, LOOK-
ing down at the Mexican hairless's body laid out on a
metal table in front of Dorothy's cage. "What happened?"

"One minute she was hiccupping, the next dead," says
the medical student. "Dr. Rush and I tried to revive her,
but she never woke up."

"She died from all the hysteria," diagnoses the orderly.
"It was too much for her."

"Poor baby."

"How do you tell someone their dog is dead?" asks the
medical student, picking up the wall phone. "I've never
done this before."

"You just say it," says the nurse.

"Hello, I'm calling from the veterinarian hospital. I'm
so sorry to tell you this, but Lupita is gone . . . We're not
sure why, but most likely, the infection entered her blood-
stream and her heart just stopped . . . Yes, the tension outside might have contributed as well."

"I told you the hysteria killed her," the orderly whispers
to the nurse.

"Yes," says the medical student, his eyes distracted and

moist, "you could call Lupita the real victim here today."
He cradles the phone. "The owner's devastated. She and
her son are going to drive in from Yonkers tomorrow to
collect the body so she can bury it in her backyard."

"I'll clean her up and call the morgue," the nurse says,
patting the student's shoulder. With practiced efficiency,
she rolls the body on its side. Its stone eyes now stare
directly at Dorothy, but the nurse mercifully closes them.
Pulling a tissue out of her white pocket, she wipes the
foam off the pink lips, already beginning to grin in rigor-
mortis. She detaches the IV tube and throws away the
half-empty cloud. She opens a drawer and takes out a
square, clean incontinence pad, the same Wee Wee brand
that Dorothy uses as her emergency toilet at home. She
covers the body with it, but Dorothy's not fooled. Dorothy
knows what's under the Wee Wee pad.

Sunday Evening

FOUNTAIN OF YOUTH

"WITNESSES SWEAR THEY SAW A BOMB UNDER Pamir's coat," says the evening newscaster, a prematurely white-haired man with a ferret-like face. "Dozens of people described the exact same explosive device down to the number of dynamite sticks and the detonator button's color. Now the mayor tells us Pamir never had a bomb. Was it a mass hallucination? What did these witnesses really see?" he asks his guest, an intense, thin woman with flyaway hair captioned, "Author of Mass Hysteria."

"It's called eyewitness disorder."

"Next they'll concoct a pill for it," Alex says.

He and Ruth are seated on their sofa, waiting for their Chinese food to arrive. Lily had woken them from their nap to tell them to stay by the phone this evening: she thinks she has another offer.

Ruth is only half listening. She's mentally arranging the furniture in their future living room and then imagining her and Alex sitting just as they are now, but instead of facing the television, they're looking at the bookcases. She can almost see the spines of her library arranged alphabetically, floor to ceiling. Finding a home for her books is no less important to Ruth than finding a museum for his paintings is to Alex.

"If eyewitness disorder is all they could come up with for a lead story," Alex says, "it must mean things are returning to normal. Maybe we'll get our asking price."

"I'll be glad if we can just get nine fifty."

She tries to get back to her daydream—or whatever it was—but after Alex distracted her, her daydream changed: she and Alex are still facing the bookcases, but now they're a *very* elderly couple sitting on their ancient plaid sofa in an unfamiliar living room. This will be where, most likely, one of them will sit alone after the other's gone, because in the end, Ruth knows, an elevator isn't a fountain of youth.

"Stay tuned," says the newscaster, "next up, the results of tonight's poll *Did the Media Go too Far?* and an exclusive interview with Pamir's girlfriend from rehab, Debbie Twitchell."

"Rahim's wife was right all along," Alex says. "The born-again wasn't his hostage, she was his lover."

The buzzer sounds.

"The Chinese is here."

Alex rises to get his wallet from the bedroom, while Ruth attends to the intercom. She presses talk, "Hello." She presses listen, but all she hears is a blasting boom box on the street: the suburban teenagers must be back. "We're on the fifth floor," she shouts to the deliveryman, and presses door. Before she answers the knock, she peers through the peephole. At first, she doesn't recognize the two women—one tall and one short—but she immediately recognizes Harold. He now sports a crimson vest, the brightest spot in the fish-eyed hallway.

Opening the door, Ruth expects Harold to bound past her and lunge at Dorothy's toys as he had yesterday, but Harold's like a different dog—composed, pensive, a serious young gentleman in a fitted red vest that reads, *Seeing Eye Puppy in Training*.

"We hope you don't mind our dropping by like this. We were out training Harold in the park," says the short, dreamy one.

"We're here to make an offer," says the tall, aloof one.

Alex comes out of their bedroom, wallet in hand. "Come in," he says.

"Can I get you something to drink?" Ruth asks. "Perhaps a bowl of water for Harold?"

"We don't want to intrude," says the short one, though Ruth can see how badly she wants to come in.

"Our bid," says the tall one, holding out an envelope. "We ask you once again to make this a sealed auction."

"My wife and I discussed this. No silent auction."

"It's as high as we can go," says the short one, looking at Ruth beseechingly.

Alex takes the envelope.

"Is it okay to pet him?" Ruth asks.

"Not while he's wearing his vest," says the tall one.

"He's still learning the difference between play and work," explains the short one.

"He's so well-behaved. Our little dog is out of control."

"How's she doing?"

"She's coming home from the hospital tomorrow. You've done a remarkable job training Harold. Maybe you can teach me a few tricks to get Dorothy to behave." As soon as she says it, Ruth regrets it. Those dreamy, pleading eyes have misinterpreted her: she thinks Ruth has made a promise of some kind, when Ruth was only making small talk.

"We can come by one evening this week. Harold's a very special boy." At the sound of his name, Harold looks up at his mistress with fidelity and awe.

"It's our final offer," interrupts the tall one, giving a quick, sharp tug on Harold's lead. Obediently, he rises to his feet.

"Good night," says the short one, slipping Ruth a second envelope. "Here's our letter in case there's a tie. I hope you'll read it."

"Good luck," Ruth calls after them as they head down the stairwell, though she knows luck will have nothing to do with it.

Before they open the envelope to see what the offer is, Alex calls Lily to check if breaking the seal commits them in any way to a silent auction.

The buzzer sounds. They forgot all about the Chinese food. "I'll get it," Ruth says, leaving Alex alone in the living room.

"We're on the fifth floor," she shouts into the intercom, and then waits for the deliveryman at the stairwell's summit. As he makes his slow ascent, Ruth tries to guess what the ladies' offer might be. It has to be more substantial than their last bid of nine hundred thousand made at the height of the threat. Nine twenty-five? Nine fifty? Ruth can smell the garlic shrimp as the deliveryman trudges up the last flight. His ears are bright red from bicycling in the cold; his face is sweaty from the steam heat and the exertion. He has to be in his late fifties, bringing her and Alex their dinner in subzero weather, and she was worried that nine hundred thousand wasn't enough? When his blood-less fingers count out her change, nine dollars, she says, "Keep it, please."

"Nine hundred and fifty thousand," Alex says as she walks in, a bag of Chinese food in each hand. She wishes she could put down her load and embrace him, but the garlic sauce is beginning to leak. "Is Lily calling Harold's ladies to tell them the good news or should we?"

"She's calling the Parkas and Yellow Rubbers to see if they'll make a counteroffer." The phone rings: Alex an-swers, listens, and says, "Tell them they can go to hell."

Ruth hurries into the kitchen, abandons the dripping bags in the sink, and picks up the cordless.

"I was just telling Alex that the Parkas have tried to pull a fast one again," Lily says. "They offered nine hundred and fifty-one thousand."

"They can keep their lousy thousand," Ruth says.

"Dr. Gilbert will be e-mailing you her offer shortly," Lily says.

"Who's Dr. Gilbert?" Ruth asks.

"Yellow Rubbers. She wants to include a letter. After the Parkas' antics, I reminded her that we're only accept-ing bids in increments of five thousand dollars. Should I call Harold's Ladies to see if they want to stay in the ring?"

Ruth is still worried that she'd inadvertently made some kind of promise to the beseeching eyes. "I suppose it can't hurt, but the short one said it's the best that they can do and I believe her."

"Why don't we give them until tomorrow morning to see if they can't do a little better," Lily says.

"Tell them they should go through you, Lily," Alex adds. "I don't want them coming by again."

After they hang up, Ruth asks, "You think they really would have come by?"

"For our apartment, they were ready to teach Dorothy to behave."

Ruth rescues what's left of their shrimp and vegetables. The carton has almost bled out in the sink. When all eight shrimp are safely in a bowl, she sits at the kitchen table and takes out the second envelope. It's been in her robe pocket since the short one had slipped it to her. Before Alex went off to wake the computer and check for Dr. Gilbert's e-mail, he'd warned Ruth not to read it, but she feels obligated. At the very least, she'd promised the short one that she'd read their letter. She opens the envelope; it's barely adhered, as if someone had only kissed the glue for luck before sealing it.

> *Dear Mr. and Mrs. Cohen,*
> *First of all, we want to tell you how sorry we are to*
> *hear about your little dog's back troubles. We wish her*
> *our very best.*
>
> *If you should choose us in the event of a tie, we will*
> *cherish your apartment. We love the original ironwork*
> *on the entry door and the windowed kitchen, but that's*
> *not why you should choose us. My partner, Millicent,*
> *and I have raised five Seeing Eye dogs in training:*

Harold is our sixth. One of the few places a Seeing Eye puppy in training is allowed off-leash is a dog park. Being only a block away from Tompkins Square's beautiful one would mean the world to us. Harold will be leading a visually impaired person soon enough, it would be so wonderful if he could run free.

Warmly, Judy

She carries the letter into the bedroom intending to read it aloud to Alex, and then argue that they should accept the ladies' offer and be happy with nine fifty. All they wanted was an elevator, and now they have one.

He looks up from the computer screen. "Nine hundred and sixty thousand. Let's grab it, Ruth."

She slips the letter back into her pocket. "What about Harold's Ladies?"

"You heard the tall one, nine fifty is their final offer."

"We promised they had until morning. We have to give them a chance. What did the doctor's letter say?"

"I didn't read it," Alex says, rising from his chair to find the source of the garlic scent.

Ruth sits down at the computer.

Dear Seller,

I'm forty-eight years old, single, with no pets. I like the East Village because it's close to my work. I'm a chiropractor. I also do Indian head massage and reflexology. I'm quiet; I never have parties and will make a good neighbor.

Sincerely,

Dr. Katherine Gilbert

She wishes she hadn't read either letter, the petless chiropractor's or the one in her pocket, heavy as a stone. She reads the doctor's e-mail again, hoping to see something she'd missed before, something poignant and unspoken beneath the lines—*Grandpa's ailing and the flour bins are empty*—but all Ruth can glean from the sad letter is that Dr. Gilbert doesn't own a cow.

Alex samples a shrimp as he sets the table—the good dishes and cloth napkins. He opens a new bottle of wine. He plans to toast their future happiness though he's a little disappointed they didn't get their asking price. He wanted to be a millionaire, if only for the minute or two it took him to write Lily's commission check and then give the rest to the sellers. He looks around for a candle to make the celebration especially festive and romantic, but all he finds is a sickeningly perfumed aromatherapy candle Ruth's sister sent her and a Yahrzeit candle he forgot to light for his dead father. He peels off the Hebrew sticker, sets the glass of wax on the table, like a candelabrum, and lights the virgin wick, but when the flame comes to life, the setting looks more mournful than romantic. He can't help but remember his father, the immigrant shoe salesman who revered millionaires. Before calling Ruth for dinner, he goes into the bathroom, opens the medicine cabinet, and takes a Viagra in case the celebration continues. When he returns to the kitchen, it's as if his father is sitting there, joining them for dinner. He douses the overhead fluorescent to reset the mood with soft candlelight, but now the dark kitchen is peopled with more ghosts—his mother, his younger brother, his favorite aunt, an artist friend who hung himself, the German soldier he killed with his knife.

Ruth turns on the light. "Why is it so dark in here?" Then she sees the candle and the wine, and shuts it again.

Alex pours them both a glass as Ruth sits down. "To Dorothy," he says.

They clink rims.

"To our beautiful new home," Ruth says.

"And to Yellow Rubbers for making it possible," Alex adds. He waits for Ruth to toss back her wine as she does when she feels victorious, but she merely takes a sip, as if it were bitter medicine.

"You don't feel bad about Millicent and Judy?"

"Who?"

"Harold's Ladies. They really want our apartment. Did you know Harold is their sixth Seeing Eye puppy?"

"I told you not to read the letter, Ruth."

"I wish I hadn't."

He reaches across the table and caresses her hand. He wants her tonight; he needs to hold something warm and alive that he loves to dispel the ghosts.

"The ladies might come up with another ten," she says, oblivious to his touch. "Even if they can come up with five more, let's consider it, Alex. We should do the right thing and give it to Harold's Ladies."

"You want us to give away ten thousand dollars?" he says, releasing her hand.

"I don't know."

"Why is giving away ten grand the right thing, Ruth?"

"From the moment Lily told us what our apartment was worth, we've thought of little else but money."

"Is that such a crime? What about us? Ten thousand

dollars will pay for our move: forty-five years of paintings, forty-five years of books. You want us to carry it all downstairs, one box at a time?"

"For a million dollars, we wished a suicide bomber on Baltimore."

"We were scared like everyone else. Nobody wished a bomb on Baltimore."

"I did," she says.

"Oh, for God's sakes, Ruth! We're talking about ten thousand dollars!"

Alex finishes his dinner in silence, and then disappears into his studio, slamming the door. Ruth is tempted to follow him to try to win the argument—*We got lucky today only because the city was terrified; Shouldn't we share our good fortune?* But had he said yes, would she really give up ten thousand dollars so that Harold could have a dog park?

She blows out the Yahrzeit candle and can't help but remember her parents—the deeply religious egg-peddler who refused to make an extra nickel off the war's black market and her pragmatic, embittered mother.

She goes into their bedroom and lies down, getting under the covers as if she's coming down with a fever. It takes her a moment or two to realize what, exactly, she's burning up with—shame. She's no more willing to give up ten thousand dollars than anyone else. There you have it, she's ashamed to be human.

Under a cone of incandescence, Alex's hair is as white as a barrister's wig. He sits at his worktable, arguing in his head with Ruth—*Ten thousand was your salary for years; Ten thousand dollars was more than I earned for four years of combat; We can't move without help.* He looks around his studio at what he'll be moving—stacks of FBI memos, flat files heavy with prints, a palette table mountainous with dried paint, racks of paintings. Even if he hires men to bubble-wrap the paintings, no one can help him with the herculean task of deciding what to discard and what to keep, what was worth the effort and what wasn't, who he was and who he isn't.

He opens his paint jars with new urgency. Page fifty-one still needs illuminating. Employing the stencil he finished cutting two nights ago, he begins ornamenting the manuscript's border, his brush wet with cadmium red. The FBI memo at the center of this collage is especially beautiful—the blacked-out shapes are like tire marks on snow. He reads between the marks. *Cohen née Kushner, Ruth (b. 1930) Arrested November 15, 1954, disobeying court order: marching without a permit: Citizens Against the H-Bomb. January 26, 1955, at 1:55 p.m., informant observed subject, Ruth Cohen, speaking at a rally against the Korean War. Subject, Ruth Cohen, suspended for six months without pay for refusing to cooperate with the House Un-American Activities Committee.* She hasn't changed. He visualizes a portrait of Ruth—on the kind side of middle-age, sporting her red cat-eye glasses and crowned by wild black defiant hair—in the only blank area left to do on page fifty-one, but before he can capture her in paint, the image dissolves into what it is—an old man's memory. Yet it's not nostalgia he feels; it's arousal.

.   .   .

Alex's body heat wakens Ruth. She must have dozed off reading. Her glasses are still on. Her *Portable Chekhov* presses on her chest, as heavy as a brick. Alex is naked and erect. Only as he envelops her, does she realize that he must have taken a Viagra with dinner (he needs to take it with food) and their fight ruined the evening. Either he's forgiven her or, just as likely, he can't bear to waste the pill, let alone such a triumphant erection. She pulls her nightgown free of her arms and head and flings it into the night.

DOROTHY HIDES IN THE BACK OF HER CAGE. A hypnotic, alarming odor is escaping from under the Wee Wee pad. Normally, when Dorothy smells death—a run-over squirrel, a squashed baby bird—she yearns to roll upon it and perfume her fur, but this is different. This smells like something that will never wash off.

"What's the body still doing here?" asks the nurse, as she carries in a new patient, a beagle with three legs and a bandaged stump.

"No more cooler space," answers the orderly. "Tito from the morgue says he's never seen anything like it and he's been here twenty years. We lost eight dogs, six cats, and an iguana this afternoon."

"At least take her out in the hall. How would you like to sleep next to a corpse?" says the nurse.

The orderly puts on rubber gloves, lest the smell get on his skin, and removes the Wee Wee pad. Dorothy's view is unobstructed. The corpse's grin is now a grimace; the lidded eye sockets have sunken like potholes. The gloves slide death off the table and carry it away.

The air immediately freshens. Dorothy turns in a circle, as if she were making a bed in tall meadow grass rather than on a hard cage floor. She curls up as best she can, but she can't find a comfortable position: she's too despondent. She misses her spot on the big bed, Alex in the middle, she and Ruth on either side.

Monday Morning

ANIMAL SENSE

RUTH REACHES FOR HER GLASSES BUT THEY aren't on the nightstand. She squints at the floor, straining to see if they fell during the night. The sun hasn't yet cleared the chimneys. She can barely distinguish carpet from floor.

"What's going on?" Alex asks.

"I can't find my glasses."

Getting up, he walks naked to Ruth's side, eases himself onto his knees, and looks under the bed, while Ruth suddenly remembers where her glasses were last—on her forehead, before she and Alex made love.

"Do you see them?" she asks.

"Not yet," he says, hunting behind the nightstand. He finds a nickel and a length of dental floss, but no glasses.

She palpates the bedcovers, roots between the sheets, gropes under the pillows. Finally, her fingers feel the thick plastic temples wedged between the headboard and the mattress. Careful not to pull too hard, lest something snap, she excises her frames from the crevasse and lifts them into the daylight. They are miraculously undamaged, save for a missing lens.

"I found them," she tells Alex, who is still on his knees, hunting. "The right lens fell out. Do you see it anywhere? Look near the headboard."

She puts on her glasses to help search, too, but rather than one eye of clarity, she gets two eyes of disorientation. A moment later, Alex holds up what Ruth assumes is her lens. She offers him the one-eyed frames. "Can you fix it?"

"I can try. Where's your other pair?"

"This is my other pair."

In the kitchen, showered and dressed, Alex tries stubbornly to repair her glasses (no matter how much tape he employs, the lens keeps popping out), while Ruth, still in her robe, puts up the kettle. Despite the fact she's boiled water in this exact spot for forty-five years, without her glasses she feels vulnerable and baffled and oddly suspicious of yesterday's good fortune, and then she remembers that the ladies' letter is still in her pocket.

"Let's give the ladies a little while longer, at least until we get back from the hospital." But Ruth knows her benevolence is such a tiny gesture, like a rich man buying a dollar raffle ticket for a good cause.

Ruth fetches Dorothy's blanket, while Alex looks for his gloves. She wears her glasses, despite the dizzying sensation of seeing half the world in clarity and half in speculation. Before they leave the apartment, she checks with Alex, "You have your hearing aids? I've only got one good eye today." At the top of the spiral staircase, she takes his arm and says, "Don't run down, Alex, stay with me." Even though she's walked down those steps for four and a half decades, with one lens in and one lens out, she feels as if she's descending Mount Zion.

In the cab, on the ride uptown, she finally takes off her glasses to rest her eyes. Outside her window, the city is but light and shadow. Stopped for a signal (she has no idea where) she hears a siren on her left, then another on her right, then a third up ahead, and a fourth behind her, as if inciting one another to howl like neighborhood dogs.

"You hear that?" she asks Alex.

"I don't hear anything," he says.

"Turn up your hearing aids."

"I hear them," the cabbie says.

Ruth slips her glasses back on to peer outside. Better one eye than none. To give her good eye the best advantage, she rolls down the tinted, streaked window. The signal changes and cold air rushes in. It feels especially harsh and biting against her naked, blind eye. The wind sets Alex's hearing aids to whistling. He looks around, lost, deaf to everything but that thrilling note. She closes the window. An elevator may not be a fountain of youth, but it's an elevator.

"Is something happening?" Alex asks her.

"Let's go get our dog, Alex. There will always be something happening," she says.

In front of the hospital, Alex helps her out of the cab. She doesn't entirely trust her perceptions. The curb looks both near and far.

She and Alex present their picture IDs to a new guard, a short fat woman whose tight, leather walkie-talkie holster looks like a string tying together two sausages. Alex goes through the metal detector first, waits for Ruth on the far side.

As she starts through the gate, without depth perception, she feels like a camel trying to fit through the eye of a needle.

In the crowded waiting room, Alex gets in line to inform the receptionist that he and Ruth are here to pick up Dorothy, while Ruth sits down on the only vacant chair. To her left is a thin man with a limp rabbit saddled over his knees and to her right is a woman whose eyes are such a bright red from crying that the rims look as if they're bleeding. A stoic, stricken boy of about twenty, probably her son, walks toward her, holding out a cafeteria tray draped over with a Wee Wee pad. No one has to tell Ruth what's underneath. She takes off her glasses. She prefers light and shadow. But even without glasses, she can still distinguish Alex amid the blur of beasts and men, his unstoppable feet tapping as he waits to take their dog home.

DOROTHY KNOWS ALEX AND RUTH ARE NEARBY. She doesn't guess it; she doesn't wish it—she *knows* it. Wet nose to the bars, she stands at her cage door, and calls for them as loudly as she can, so they can find her. Her ward-mates, the pug and the beagle, join in. To lift her voice above the trio, Dorothy barks in falsetto. One door down, a Great Dane, a Saint Bernard, and a pit bull add their baritones. Then a basset hound howls and the beagle bays and a Pomeranian yaps until, all up and down the corridor, the patients find their voices.

"Why are they going crazy again?" says the orderly wheeling a food cart behind the nurse. "You think something new happened, they know something we don't?"

"They know it's time for breakfast," the nurse says.

9 780307 386786